JEWISH

Love

STORIES FOR KIDS

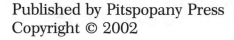

Published by Pitspopany Press
Copyright © 2002

Cover Design by Ben Gasner Studios
Book Design by Tiffen Studios (T.C. Peterseil)

Pitspopany Press titles may be purchased for fundraising programs by schools and organizations by contacting:

Marketing Director, Pitspopany Press
40 East 78th Street, Suite 16D
New York, New York 10021
Tel: (800) 232-2931
Fax: (212) 472-6253
Email: pitspop@netvision.net.il

ISBN: 0-930143-14-1   Cloth
ISBN: 0-930143-15-X   Paper

Printed in Israel

TABLE OF CONTENTS

OTHER BOOKS IN THIS SERIES:

JEWISH HUMOR STORIES FOR KIDS

JEWISH SCI-FI STORIES FOR KIDS

JEWISH DETECTIVE STORIES FOR KIDS

JEWISH LOVE STORIES FOR KIDS

THE PURR-FECT CAT

by Leslie Cohen

Leslie Cohen

I was born and raised in New York City and now live with my husband and our three "sabras" on Kibbutz Ein Hashofet in Israel.

I started my career as a writer by writing short stories for children. These stories have been published in various magazines in Israel and abroad, including the popular "Cricket" magazine in the USA, and the prize-winning multicultural magazine, "Stepping Stones."

Recently, I published my first book, a collection of poems and short stories called "Facets of the Poet."

THE PURR-FECT CAT

I learned from my best friend, Davey, that all beginnings are difficult – not just my own.

Until the day I met Davey, my life was a nightmare. My earliest memory is of feeling cold and miserably hungry. I was wedged between my brothers and sisters, and every one of us was crying. Mama must have died a few days after she gave birth to us. I remember her soft voice and her warm caress, but I never actually saw her, since a cat's eyes don't open for about a week after it's born. Gradually, the crying stopped and I was all alone. I don't even know if any of my siblings survived.

I had nobody to look after me, or even care what happened to me. As soon as I could see clearly enough to search for food, I sniffed around the garbage bins. But even when I found food, I had to fight off other animals in order to get enough to eat. Most of them were much bigger and stronger than I, but I was determined to survive.

At night, when I tried to sleep, I was never sure what might happen. I lived by my wits, surviving on scraps of rotting food, until one cold and rainy day a big dog snapped at my back left paw. Somehow, I managed to climb a tree, and stayed there all night

and the following day. If I hadn't been starving, I might still be up that tree!

The next day, although the weather was just as miserable, my luck changed for the better. Just before twilight, a young boy approached me, speaking to me in a soft and gentle tone of voice. I didn't understand what he was saying, but I could sense that he was very kind. I was just as starved for companionship as I was for food, so I followed him slowly down the hill to the door of his house.

From outside the kitchen window, he called, "Mom, come and see!"

Almost immediately, a woman came outside. She looked startled when she saw me, and said, "Poor little kitten – its leg is all bloody!"

"Can we keep it?" Davey pleaded.

"Keep it?" She repeated, sounding nervous. "I hardly think so! I've never had a pet and I wouldn't know what to do with it. And, anyway, it looks pretty sickly to me."

"Yeah, it does," Davey agreed. "That's why I brought it home. I thought maybe I could take care of it – at least give it some milk."

"Where did you find it?"

"It was hanging around the garbage cans, looking for food. Could we keep it, at least for a while?"

"Let's wait and see what your father says when he gets home."

"Okay," said Davey, "but in the meantime let's give it some milk – it looks so hungry!" he pleaded.

Davey's mother, Miriam, nodded and they went indoors together.

"Don't worry, I'll be right back," Davey assured me. "Wait for me right here on the patio."

And, in less than a minute, he was back outside, holding a small plastic saucer.

"Here's some milk for you. Why don't you come and drink it? I can see you're hungry," he said, putting the saucer on the pavement. "Don't be afraid. If my parents let me keep you, I'll give you milk every day," he assured me, in a kind and caring tone of voice.

Davey crouched near me while I tasted the delicious, creamy milk, but he didn't touch me. I lapped up the milk, feeling extremely grateful for this wonderful treatment.

A few minutes later, Miriam came back outside. She bent over to get a closer look at me, but, unlike Davey, she avoided touching me.

"This cat has a serious problem," she said, pointing to my back leg.

"Of course it has a problem – that's why it needs me," Davey answered.

"I see what you mean," Miriam said. She looked back and forth between Davey and me for a

minute or two and then suggested: "Let's find a box for the kitten and bring it inside. After all, it's cold and nasty out here."

This was my first time inside a house, and it felt warm and pleasant.

"Maybe we should wrap the back leg with a rag," Miriam suggested.

"Of course we should!" said Davey, and quickly added, "I'll do it myself."

And he was so gentle that it didn't hurt at all. In fact, it felt good.

Davey and I sat on the warm, thick rug on the living room floor. Davey had been building a city out of blocks, and he sat me on his lap, stroking my bony back, while he explained all the different parts of the city to me. The longer he spoke, the more easily I understood the words he was using. Soon English became my own language.

It was getting dark when the front door opened and a little girl skipped inside.

"What's that?" she asked, pointing at me.

"Come and take a look," Davey told her. "There's nothing to be afraid of. It's just a baby kitten that I found on my way home from school. I'm hoping Mom and Dad will let me keep it for a pet."

Davey's five-year-old sister, Sarah, giggled when she touched my fur. "Ooh, it's soft!" she exclaimed, grabbing my tail.

"Careful not to touch the back leg!" Miriam

warned her.

Sarah wanted to play with me, but Miriam said she had to have a bath and dinner first, so I was left alone with Davey again. He talked to me while he added a new building to his city. "This is a pet hospital," he explained. "They take sick cats there and make them well. I think every city should have one."

Another relaxing hour passed before Davey's father, Michael, came home. It was dark outside when the front door creaked open and Davey ran to greet him, carrying me.

"Dad, look at this little gray kitten that followed me home today. Isn't it cute? Do you think we can keep it?" he asked, holding me up to show his father.

"It doesn't look like this poor little kitten has much of a chance," said Michael, examining me carefully. I could see where Davey's gentleness had come from. "We can go to the vet for a professional opinion, but I'm almost certain he's going to have to put it to sleep."

A neighbor came to baby-sit for Sarah, and Michael helped Davey put me in a large box, with a soft, old towel beneath me. Davey carried me outside to the car. He sat in the back seat with my box on his lap, talking to me all the way to the vet's office. As we passed his school and other familiar buildings in the area, he told me a little about each one, as if he wanted to introduce me to the whole neighborhood.

There were a few people ahead of us in the reception room, and Davey kept petting me and whispering to me while we waited. "Don't be scared of the doctor," he told me. "He knows how to take care of cats, and I'm sure he won't hurt you."

Dr. Wexler welcomed us into the examination room and placed my box on a big table.

"Do you think we can keep it?" Davey asked, before the vet had even had a chance to look at me.

Dr. Wexler chuckled and said, "First of all, this "it" is a "she", and we'll have to take a look at her before we can decide anything."

"I think her leg is broken," Miriam said. "It was bleeding terribly when Davey brought her home."

The vet talked to me as if I were an important person. "Is it true that you really have a broken leg?" he asked, letting me out of the box so I could walk on the examination table. Realizing I was free, I leaped down and ran around the room. Even though my back leg still hurt, I hadn't felt this good in a long time!

After a minute, Dr. Wexler announced his professional opinion.

"It looks to me as if this cat is a survivor," he said. "She's been living on her own for a while and she obviously knows how to take care of herself. It's true that her paw is badly bruised and she may never

learn to walk steadily, but her leg isn't broken. In fact, with proper care and attention, I predict it will heal very nicely."

"What do you mean?" Michael asked the vet. "She can barely walk!"

"That's true. She limps when she tries to walk, but she can run and jump just fine. I would guess she's been dragging her hind leg and holding her paw upside down because of her bruise. But with the right kind of treatment, it will heal," he repeated.

"So, can we keep her?" asked Davey.

"I've never had a pet," said Miriam, nervously. "I wouldn't know what to do with it. A cat needs special food and it would need to be trained so it won't mess up the house."

"Since Davey brought her home, she would have to be his responsibility," Michael pointed out.

"Do you think he's old enough to do everything the cat needs done for her?" Miriam asked.

"I'm nine and a half. Sure I'm old enough to take care of her!" Davey spoke up. "Why don't you give me a chance to prove it to you?"

Miriam began to relax and she even smiled as Michael asked the vet to explain all the things Davey would have to do for me.

"What about the bruised hind leg?" she asked. "How can Davey take care of that?"

"If you keep it wrapped in a bandage, with

15

antibiotic cream, it will heal. She may never walk completely straight, but you can train her to stop dragging her back paw by turning it right-side-up whenever you see her dragging it."

"I'll work with her every day," Davey promised. "If we keep her, I mean."

When he looked at his parents, his sincerity was plain to see.

"It looks like you have a junior vet here," said Dr. Wexler.

Michael picked me up and put me in Davey's arms.

"She could sleep in a box in the house, and you could let her run around outside all day," the vet suggested. "She's used to being outdoors and she's very strong, in spite of her size. In fact, my guess is that she's used to defending herself."

"How old do you think she is?" asked Miriam.

"I suppose she's about three or four months old," said the vet.

"So, does that mean we can keep her?" Davey asked, for the tenth time that day.

Miriam and Michael looked at each other. As they said "Okay" in unison, I felt my life was just beginning.

At first, Davey changed my bandage twice a day. He wrapped it very gently, assuring me every

time, "This may hurt a little bit, but it's going to make you well."

Compared to the life style I had known before, this was heavenly. I could take a nap any time I wanted to, with no fear of being attacked.

I got used to the Rosen family's routine in no time. Everybody got up early in the morning. They made so much noise it woke me out of my deep sleep and sweet dreams! But it was worth it, because every morning I awoke to the most wonderful aroma of food cooking on the stove. Miriam had bought me a special set of dishes, and, at breakfast, Davey would remind everybody, "Don't forget to leave a bite for my Kitty!"

Michael always hurried off to work before the children left. Then Sarah's friend Rachel would knock on the front door and the two girls would rush off to kindergarten. After that, Davey would set my box out on the front patio, with a small dish of milk near it.

"You won't be lonely," he always said. "I'll be back before you know it!"

The box was comfortable, but as I got stronger I wanted to run around outdoors and climb trees again, so I only used it for sleeping.

Miriam left the house much later than the others. She walked very slowly and when she came home, she got into bed to take a nap every day. She

always said, "Hello, Kitty" and "Bye-bye, Kitty," but she never bent down to pat my fur. For a long time, I thought she didn't like me as much as the others did. I was too young to realize that she was pregnant and it was hard for her to bend.

After I had been with the Rosens for a few days, Davey said, "We have to give the cat a real name. We can't just keep calling her Kitty."

"You're right," Miriam agreed. "But what kind of a name would be appropriate for a cat? I mean, I don't think it would be right to give her the same sort of name you would call a new baby, do you?"

While Davey was thinking that over, Sarah said, "Let's call her Lick-Lick!"

"Nope!" said her friend, Rachel, "You should call her Furry."

The two girls argued with each other over names for a few minutes, and then went out to play. I could see that Davey wasn't paying much attention to their suggestions.

"I wish you could tell us what you want us to call you," Davey whispered to me, looking straight into my eyes.

But I had never had a name, and I had no idea what I wanted to be called.

The next day, Davey came home from school all excited. "I have the perfect name for my kitten!" he told Miriam. "This morning we were learning songs for Passover and there's a cat in one of them –

it's called *Shunra.*"

"Shunra!" said Miriam. "Of course! That's the cat in *Had Gadya*, the song we sing on Passover. Did the rabbi tell you that Shunra is the Aramaic word for cat? You're right – it is the perfect name!" she agreed.

Davey sat on the living room floor with me and explained who Shunra was.

"Shunra was a very special cat in Jewish history," he explained, "and I think you should be named after someone special – someone like you."

So, that's how I came to have a name, and it made me feel very important. Even Sarah and Rachel agreed it was a good name for me. When Davey explained to them it was from the song in the Passover *Haggadah*, they started singing the song and giggling. Those two giggled about everything, anyway.

I noticed that Sarah and Rachel spent a lot of time together. After kindergarten, they would play outside until it was dark, then Sarah would go to Rachel's house or Rachel would come to our house. Sometimes another girl played with them, too. It seemed like they giggled as much as they talked, and they talked a lot! But I never saw Davey play with anybody. He just went to school every day and came home and played with me, or built something with his blocks. He didn't giggle like the girls, either.

My first Passover stands out clearly in my memory. About a week before the holiday began, Miriam told Davey, "Now that you've shown us how grown up and responsible you are, I want you to read from the Haggadah."

"But I never did that before!" said Davey. "And you know how much trouble I have reading Hebrew," he added.

"You should say 'used to have,'" said Miriam, "because I've noticed that since you've been taking care of Shunra, you've been reading your Hebrew lessons aloud to her, and I can hear how much you've improved."

"So you really think I can do it?" Davey sounded very proud.

"Without a doubt," Miriam said. "I think you're ready to read the part about the plagues."

"I'll be the youngest reader at the *seder*," Davey pointed out.

"That's right," said Miriam. "But, since you're mature enough to take care of a crippled kitten, I'm sure you're old enough to read at the seder."

Miriam handed Davey a Haggadah with portions marked off for him to read in Hebrew. He sat down next to me to practice, and he translated every word, showing me the pictures. Now that I understood English perfectly well, I was beginning to

learn Hebrew as well. Davey patiently explained the story of Passover to me, and told me about the Exodus from Egypt.

"The Jews were slaves of the Pharaoh, who was the ruler of Egypt," he told me. "After Pharaoh tried to kill the boy babies in every Jewish family, our great leader, Moses, knew it was time for the Jews to escape. So he instructed everybody to pack their things, and he led our people across the Red Sea, to freedom."

Davey also explained that the Haggadah was the story of the flight from Egypt. "Every Passover, Jews all over the world read the Haggadah at the seder – the Feast of Liberty."

Davey also told me about his family, most of whom I hadn't met yet. His mother's parents, Grandma Shulamith and Grandpa Aaron, lived too far away to come for the seder. But Michael's parents and his younger brother, Saul, would be there. I knew that Uncle Saul was Davey's best friend, even though he was seven years older than Davey.

On the first night of the holiday, I could hear Davey humming Passover melodies as he helped Miriam place the chairs around the table. He set my basket on the floor, where I could see everything. He was going over his reading with me when the door opened.

"So, here's the famous Shunra," said Saul, as

he entered the house. "I hear this kitten is a descendant of the original Shunra, isn't that right?" He asked, picking me up and petting me.

"Look," said Davey proudly, "her back paw has completely healed!"

Saul answered, "I'm not at all surprised. After all, you've been taking care of her like a real pro, haven't you?"

I had been with the Rosens less than a month, but already my fur was fluffy and I was feeling very fit. I played outdoors in their garden every day while Davey was in school. Miriam didn't pay much attention to me, but I noticed that my bowl was always full of fresh milk, even when Davey wasn't home.

The Passover seder lasted for many hours. After each reading, Saul turned to Davey or Sarah and asked them questions about the story of the Exodus. They tried to imagine all the things the Jewish children did to help their parents during the escape from Egypt, and the conversation at the table was lively.

Davey had told me about the *Afikomen* – the *matzah* that his father hid for the children to find later – and I noticed Michael wrapping a piece of matzah in a napkin at the beginning of the seder, when he thought nobody was looking. Later, when he excused himself to go to the bathroom, I saw him take the Afikomen with him. I followed him into the

living room and watched him hide it.

During the seder, Sarah sang the Four Questions, and when Davey read from the Haggadah, everybody praised him. I could tell he was very pleased with himself, and I was proud of him, too. Not only had he read in a clear voice, he had taught me enough Hebrew to be able to follow along!

After the story of the Exodus was read, there were games. When Sarah and Davey went to find the Afikomen, Saul said, "Let's pretend this is the desert, and the Afikomen is hidden in an oasis."

Saul tied bandanas around Davey's and Sarah's heads, and gave them each a walking stick. The two of them went around the living room, pretending they were searching for the Afikomen in the desert. When Sarah found it, she and Davey each got a present from Grandpa.

Then everybody sang songs. When they got to the *Had Gadya*, Davey told the family that I was named for Shunra, the cat in the story. He also told them that the rabbi in school had explained how God gave all creatures – including cats, not just people – a mission in life. I wondered what mine might be.

The singing went on for a very long time. I dozed off listening to the happy sounds of my new family, knowing I must be about the luckiest creature in the whole world, and wondering when I was going to find out what my special task in life was.

That night I slept at the foot of Davey's bed, as I had been doing since my paw had healed. In the middle of the night, I was awakened by the sound of voices. By the time I crept into the living room, all of the adults were there and they were all talking at the same time. Michael was holding a suitcase and telling everybody to keep calm. Miriam was sprawled in a chair, looking very nervous. A few minutes later, Michael and Miriam left the house. I jumped up onto the kitchen window ledge and watched as their car pulled off.

Saul noticed me, and picked me up. "Poor thing," he said, sleepily stroking my fur. "Did we wake you up with all of our noise?" He asked me, yawning. He carried me back to Davey's room, where I curled up at the foot of the bed and went back to sleep, wondering if this was a part of Passover that Davey had forgotten to tell me about.

By the time I awoke the following morning, everybody else was up. As soon as I entered the living room, Davey picked me up and set me on his lap. "Shunra," he said, "you'll never guess what's happening to our family right now!"

I blinked and waited for him to continue. He always seemed to know what was on my mind.

"Mom went to the hospital in the middle of the night to give birth!" he said, excitedly. "It was a big surprise – we weren't expecting her to have the baby for another month."

That day was very busy in the Rosen household. Davey took me outside to play in the garden, saying, "Everybody has a lot of chores to do, so you'll be better off out here."

He put a bowl of milk for me on the patio and assured me, "Don't worry – I'll let you know what's going on!"

True to his word, he came out with a snack for me a little while later. "I've been helping the grown-ups clean the house. Grandma and Grandpa can't believe how many household chores I can do on my own," he told me.

I knew how much he helped Miriam around the house, so I wasn't at all surprised.

All morning, I could hear that the atmosphere in the house was lively. And I, too, was very excited about having a new baby in the family. I wondered if it would be a girl or a boy, and if the baby would become my friend, too, like Davey. But, as the afternoon stretched out, the house became very quiet. Grandma and Grandpa took a nap, and Sarah went to Rachel's house. Davey brought me inside to play with him and Saul on the living room floor. I listened to their quiet conversation and learned a lot about the Rosen family. Saul was telling Davey about his many cousins who lived too far away to visit. Davey and Saul planned to send greetings to each of those cousins, and let them know about the new baby.

"We should send them some pictures of you and Shunra, too," said Saul. "I bet your cousins would like to hear about how you took care of her and saved her life."

They were still making plans late that afternoon, when Michael arrived home looking weary but very happy, too.

"It's a girl!" he announced, excitedly. "Miriam had to have an operation, but everything is fine now," he said.

Everybody started talking all at once, and Davey held me in his arms, hugging and stroking me for a long time.

"Shunra, you've got a new baby sister," he whispered in my ear. "Someone else to love you."

Because the baby had been born almost a whole month early, she was very small and would have to stay in an incubator for a week.

Grandma and Grandpa and Saul slept over again that night, and Saul stayed with us until Miriam and the baby could come home from the hospital. Meanwhile, the whole family was busy preparing for the new baby. Her room needed furniture, and she needed clothes.

For a few days, there were neighbors all over the house, bringing cakes, trays of food, and presents for Davey and Sarah and the new baby. Davey was in and out of the house all day, running errands. I had never seen him so busy. Between chores, he took

time out to explain to me everything that was going on. Having a baby was a big event, I realized.

"Davey helped us just like a grown-up," Michael told Miriam on the day she came home with the baby. "It looks as if taking care of Shunra has taught him to be responsible for all sorts of things!" Davey beamed with joy at the compliment.

"Mom and Devorah had a very hard time in the hospital," Davey told me, "so they need a lot of sleep to make up for it now."

And they did sleep a lot. Miriam's parents, Grandma Shulamith and Grandpa Aaron, arrived right after Passover. They took care of the house and spent time with Davey and Sarah. Grandma and Grandpa were very kind to me, and they told Davey they thought his having me for a pet was a wonderful thing.

For a long time after Devorah was born, Miriam was very tired and needed a lot of help around the house. Sarah was too little to help, and anyway, she was always busy with her friend Rachel, so Davey became Miriam's special assistant. Every day after school, he went to the store and, when he got back, helped Miriam clean the house. But Davey still had time to play with me, and to read to me in Hebrew. He got into the habit of going over his lessons with me. As I picked up the Hebrew

27

language, I began to learn Hebrew proverbs and sayings. The first one Davey taught me was: "All beginnings are difficult." He explained that everything seems hard if you've never done it before – like learning a new language, or even playing a game for the first time.

While Davey was at school, I thought about the saying, "All beginnings are difficult." My life had been awfully hard at the beginning, but from the day I met Davey, everything changed. Davey told me that God makes every creature for a reason. Was it Davey's purpose in life to rescue me? It certainly seemed that way. I kept wondering what my special mission in life might be, and how I was going to find out.

"Summer vacation is beginning in a few weeks," Davey told me one day. "My birthday is in summer, and we always have a party," he added. I could tell he was looking forward to it.

But, early that summer, Devorah got sick. One morning, while Davey and I were playing in the living room, Miriam said to Davey, "I have to take Devorah to the doctor. Can I leave you in charge of the house while I'm gone?"

"Of course," he answered. "What do I have to do?"

"Just straighten things up a little," said Miriam. "The most important thing is to answer the phone whenever it rings, and take messages. If anybody in the family calls, tell them I took Devorah

to the doctor and I'll call them back later."

Michael was at work and Sarah was at Rachel's house, so Davey and I stayed alone all morning. The first time the phone rang, it was Miriam.

"The doctor says Devorah needs to go to the hospital for tests," she told him, "so Grandma and Grandpa and Saul are coming to stay with you and Sarah."

"And Shunra," Davey added, stroking my thick fur. "Don't forget she's part of the family now, too."

Davey and I were alone most of the day, and we spent a lot of time playing on the living room rug. He made himself cornflakes and milk for lunch, and he filled my bowl with milk so carefully that none of it spilled. Sarah was still out playing when the family arrived. Davey had cleaned up the living room and made his bed and Sarah's. He was washing the dishes in the kitchen sink when the door opened. Grandma and Grandpa walked around the house, exclaiming at how neat it was and what a wonderful job Davey had done on his own.

Saul said, "Let's take Shunra outside for a game of catch."

"I'm no good at playing ball," said Davey.

"But Shunra needs some exercise," Saul insisted. "She's been eating so well that she's actually getting fat!"

Davey laughed and picked me up. "Time for your exercise, Shunra," he told me. He and Saul set up a laundry basket and took turns throwing the ball into it. Every time Davey got the ball in, I got a prize. Saul had brought a bag of cat treats for me!

We played for a long time, until Grandma called us in for dinner.

"Your mother has to stay at the hospital with Devorah overnight," Grandma told us at dinner, "and your father is going there right after work. So we're staying until tomorrow."

"What's wrong with Devorah?" Davey asked.

"She has a problem with her heart," said Grandpa.

"Is it serious?" Davey sounded worried.

"We don't really know yet," Grandpa answered. "At first the doctors thought it would get better by itself, but now they think she might need an operation."

"So it is serious," Davey concluded.

"But they think they can handle it," Grandpa assured him.

"The doctors are taking good care of her," said Grandma.

I wanted to comfort the Rosens, and to remind Davey that "All beginnings are difficult," so I snuggled up to him and purred. I think he understood what I meant. After dinner, he took me to his room and told me how worried he was about

Devorah. I sat very still on his lap while he talked to me. Then Saul came in.

"Shunra seems to understand that something bad is happening," Davey told him. "Look how she stays close to me all of the time."

Saul praised me for being faithful. "A good listener can be a guy's best friend," he said.

They stayed up late, talking about Devorah's heart problem, and they included me in their conversation.

The next day, we played "Laundry Basket Basketball" again, and Miriam came home from the hospital with Devorah in the afternoon. That evening she sat with Davey and told him, "I know your birthday is coming up, but Devorah is so sick I don't think I'll be able to make you a party at home this year."

Davey looked disappointed, but Miriam continued, "Instead of that, Saul would like to take you to Legoland for the day."

"Wow! That sounds great!," said Davey, smiling. He loved building with Legos, and he had never been to Legoland, so he wasn't disappointed.

On Davey's birthday, Saul picked him up in the morning and they were gone until late that afternoon. They came back with a present for me – a small blanket that I could sleep on at the foot of Davey's bed. And Davey had made a huge many-

colored cat out of Legos.

"It took him hours to make this," Saul told the family.

"It's a companion for Shunra, for when I'm away at school," Davey said. "I'll put it on the bookshelf over my desk," he added.

"Or, you could put it in the living room," said Miriam. "I'll make space for it in the display cabinet, if you want."

Davey looked very proud.

That summer, Davey often stayed indoors, building with his blocks. But he also got to be pretty good at throwing and catching a ball. While Davey and Saul were playing, I ran alongside them, chasing the ball of yarn that Miriam had given me. Sometimes, a boy named Ronny from Davey's class came over to play ball, too. The boys were the same age, but I noticed that Ronny was a lot bigger than Davey. Saul taught Davey and Ronny the rules of different games. Several times, I heard Ronny inviting Davey to play ball with him and the other boys, but Davey always said, "Maybe next time," or, "We'll see," and he never went.

"I just know I couldn't keep up with the other boys," he confided in me, when we were alone in his room. "They're all so much bigger than I am! Ronny is Saul's neighbor, and he likes me, so he invites me to play. But I doubt the other boys would be so nice to me if I dropped the ball all of the time."

I hoped Davey would change his mind and accept Ronny's invitation just once, but he didn't.

When the summer was almost over, Devorah got sick again. This time, the doctors decided to operate, and Miriam would have to stay in the hospital with her for a few days. Devorah had a small hole in her heart, and it would be a serious operation.

The operation was a success and a few days after they came home, summer vacation ended. On the first day of school, Davey said to Miriam as he left the house, "Please talk to Shunra while I'm gone, so she doesn't get lonely."

After that, Miriam made a point of talking to me every day. "Let's do the laundry together," she would say, or, "Help me straighten up the living room," and I would keep her company while she worked around the house. She seemed to understand how I felt about loud noises because she always opened the back door for me when she vacuumed, saying, "Shunra, I think you had better go outside now. I know how much you hate the sound of the vacuum cleaner!" She made me feel like a regular member of the family.

That fall, Sarah went into first grade and Davey went up to fifth grade.

"I have to write a report on my hobby," said Davey one day.

33

"You can write about all the cities you built, and your trip to Legoland," Michael suggested.

"No, that's for little kids," said Davey. "I've got a better idea. I'm going to write about the history of cats!"

Saul took Davey to the library, and they brought home a stack of books about cats. Within a few weeks, Davey was well on his way to becoming an expert on the subject.

"Shunra, did you know there are more than thirty million cats living with families in America?" Davey asked me.

I snuggled up to him and purred. I bet none of them had it better than I did!

"People have been keeping cats as pets ever since Pharaoh's time," he said.

When I remembered Pharaoh from the story of the Exodus, I shivered! I was glad I hadn't lived back then. Davey told me that Shunra wasn't the only famous cat. There were cats in cartoons, like Garfield and Sylvester and Felix, and one very famous Cheshire cat had played an important role in a book called *Alice in Wonderland*.

"Cats can do important things, too," Davey told me. "Lots of farmers depend on them to hunt for mice and other pests. And there was one cat who actually helped invent plastic when he accidentally knocked over a jar of formaldehyde into his bowl of milk!"

Davey had a way of talking to me that made me

feel special and important. He and Saul took photographs of me for his report on the history of cats, and they showed me pictures of other cats – some famous, others just plain cute.

By the time Davey handed in his report, he knew more about cats than I did! No wonder he got an "A plus" – the highest grade in the class, and was asked to read his report in front of the whole class. He came home glowing, and he told me that a boy named Max in his class also had a cat. After that, Davey and Max became friends, and began visiting each other after school.

But while all of these good things were going on in Davey's life, things were still bad for Devorah. Miriam had to take her to the hospital a lot, and Grandma and Grandpa and Saul often came to stay in the evenings so that Michael could go to the hospital after work. It seemed like Davey's parents were hardly ever home.

"Isn't there anything the doctors can do for Devorah?" Davey asked them.

"It's hard for doctors to take care of a sick baby," Michael explained. "They think they're helping her, but since she's too little to talk, it's very hard for them to know how she feels."

"Is she going to have another operation?" He asked.

"We hope not," Michael answered, "but it's too

soon to tell."

One afternoon, the rabbi from Davey's school came to visit.

"Why is this happening to Devorah?" Davey asked him. "She's just a baby, so she never did anything bad. Why would God want to punish her by making her so sick?"

The rabbi said, "That's a very good question, Davey. And it's a question that grown-ups – even rabbis – ask, too. But we don't have the answers for the 'Why' questions, Davey," he said. "Human beings have a lot of knowledge about how things work, but we know very little about God's reasons for making bad things happen to good people."

I noticed that during the day, when Davey and Sarah were at school, the house was very quiet. Devorah stayed in her crib most of the time. Sometimes I heard Miriam crying while she was home alone with Devorah and me. Once, I tried to make her feel better by rubbing against her leg.

"Shunra," she said, picking me up. "You're such a sweet little kitten. I'm so glad we let Davey keep you," she told me.

Then, a few weeks before *Hanukkah*, Devorah started to get better. Miriam began to look happier, too. She even let Devorah out of her crib to crawl on the living room floor. I sat very still while Devorah was playing, hoping that she would touch me. When she finally did, she squealed with delight.

"Shunra's nice and fluffy," said Miriam to Devorah. And she added, "I'm so glad the two of you like each other."

During the week of Hanukkah, the Rosens invited people to the house almost every night for candle lighting. It was the first time since Passover that the house had been filled with people celebrating and having a good time. One evening, Sarah's friend Rachel came with her whole family. She had a lot of brothers and sisters! They all sang songs and played with their *dreidels*, and took turns petting me. On another evening, Davey's friend, Max, came over with his family. Like Davey, Max was the oldest child. He had three younger sisters who all paid a lot of attention to me. They tied a ribbon around my neck with a little bell on it.

"Now Shunra can answer us when we talk to her," said Rachel.

On the night that Grandma and Grandpa and Saul came to light candles, Grandma asked, "Are you sure you don't want to light candles at our house tomorrow evening, Miriam?"

"No thanks, Mom," Miriam said. "I still don't like to take Devorah out, even though she's doing much better now. I'm always afraid she'll have a problem, and I won't have the things I need to take care of her. But thank you for offering."

"Maybe by Passover she'll be able to come to

37

our house for the second seder," Grandma said.

"Let's hope so. That would be wonderful," said Miriam, happily.

By Passover, Devorah was starting to walk. She and I had become very good friends and we played on the living room rug every day. Miriam invited her parents to spend a few weeks with us, to celebrate Passover and Devorah's first birthday. Grandma Shulamith and Grandpa Aaron arrived a week before Passover. Grandma Shulamith took over the preparations. She got Sarah and Davey to help her look for all the *hametz* in the house and, together, they burned the last crumbs. Miriam and Grandma Shulamith were going to make the seder at our house, and Grandma and Grandpa Rosen and Saul were invited, of course.

That seder was very different from my first one because now I understood everything. Sarah sang the Four Questions, and Davey read a larger portion of the Haggadah in a steady and confident voice. He had changed a lot from when I first met him. He seemed to have grown a little taller, too.

Devorah's first birthday party was right after Passover, and the Rosen family invited the rabbi from Davey and Sarah's school for Devorah's birthday party. It was a very special celebration for the Rosen family. For a few minutes, Rabbi Neiman sat with Davey and Miriam in a quiet corner.

"Davey's become one of our best students this

past year," he told Miriam.

"Yes, we're certainly proud of him," said Miriam. "And he's a great help to me around the house," she added. "I think having the responsibility for taking care of a pet has made him very mature."

After the rabbi left, Miriam told Davey, "I'm proud of you! I know you understand how scared we were about Devorah, and it makes me feel good to know I can depend on you to help me. But, even so, I wish you would see more of your friend, Max. It can't be very much fun for you to spend so much time at home alone."

"But I like to be at home," Davey told her, "and anyway I'm not alone. Shunra's always with me!"

Miriam picked me up and set me on her lap. "I know how comforting it is to have a fluffy listener who purrs in agreement with everything you say. I understand why you love Shunra, Davey," she said. "I do, too."

One evening soon after that, Max came over for dinner.

"There's an animal hospital opening up in the city center," Max told Davey. "Do you want to go and see what they do there?"

"Of course!" said Davey. "I've heard of animal hospitals, but I've never been in one."

I hadn't seen Davey so excited for a long time.

Max's father took the boys to the animal hospital the next afternoon. When Davey came home that evening, he had a lot to talk about.

"Shunra, if ever you get sick, I know just where to take you!" he told me and Miriam all about the animal hospital.

"They have operating rooms, and lots of equipment – just like a real hospital," he said.

About a week later, Max came over to play with Davey. They talked a lot about the animal hospital. And, the next day, Max called.

"Mom, Max says the animal hospital needs volunteers to help with the animals after operations. Can I go?"

Miriam was pleased that Davey was taking such a great interest in the animal hospital. Max and Davey volunteered there twice a week, and Davey began reading about animals and how to take care of them. He and Max went to the library together and brought home stacks of books. Davey showed me all the pictures of animals who had their broken legs fixed.

"Shunra, if anything bad ever happens to you again, I'll know how to fix it," he assured me.

That summer, Sarah went to a day camp with Rachel, and Davey started spending more time away from home. He was volunteering at the animal

40

hospital a few times a week with Max, and playing ball with Ronny and his friends. Yet, he still made a special place for me in his life.

I felt very loved in the Rosen household. Miriam always talked to me when she was at home, and Devorah and I were becoming great friends. Even Rachel had started taking an interest in me, and brought me new ribbons for my bell on every special occasion.

In the middle of July, Davey had his birthday party at home. He invited Max, Ronny, and a few other boys from his class. Saul came, too, and organized a lot of games. That was the first time I had ever seen Davey with a group of boys his own age, and it was a lively party. I looked carefully at all the boys to see if Davey was the shortest, and it seemed as if he was almost the same height as the others.

When Miriam brought out the birthday cake, Saul took my photograph with all of the boys. Ronny said, "Every ball team needs a mascot, and Shunra can be ours!"

I wondered if that meant Davey had finally agreed to join their team. He hadn't talked to me about it, but I guessed Ronny had invited him again. Sure enough, after all the boys went home, Davey picked me up and hugged me. "Did you hear that, Shunra?" He asked excitedly. "Ronny asked me to join the team! I thought he had forgotten all about it,

but I guess I was wrong."

The boys practiced in different places each time they played. When it was their turn to come to our house, Saul and Davey made a special costume for me to wear, and set up a "Mascot's Stand" in the backyard. They put a bowl of milk and some treats out for me, and each boy petted me for good luck!

"I never thought I'd be playing on a ball team," Davey told me that night. "But Ronny says I've gotten a lot better since last summer. All that practicing with you and Saul really paid off!" He opened the door of his closet and looked at himself in the mirror. "I'm a lot taller, too," he realized. I nudged him and purred, meaning to say, "You're also a lot happier."

We both fell asleep early that night, exhausted from the excitement of the day's events.

After school began again in the fall, Davey was busier than ever before. He and Max kept volunteering at the animal hospital and he practiced with the team several times a week, too. He also studied very hard, and kept teaching me Hebrew and Jewish studies. At the end of the school year, Davey received a prize for being the top student in his class.

The following year, Davey started studying for his *Bar Mitzvah*. As usual, he always brought his lessons home and taught them to me.

"The rabbi says that a Bar Mitzvah is the whole process of learning to be an adult, not just the party at the synagogue," he told me. "And he says I've already

begun doing *mitzvot*, without even realizing it!"

I knew that mitzvot were the good deeds that Jews were supposed to do for each other, to please God. Davey explained that adopting me when I was a sickly orphan was one of his mitzvot.

I purred as loud and long as I could to tell him, "I've always known that!"

"And volunteering at the animal hospital is a mitzvah, too," he explained.

I rang my bell in agreement. Whenever Max came to visit Davey, I heard them talk about what they did for the sick animals in the hospital. Of course those things qualified as mitzvot!

Davey's *parsha* – the *Torah* portion he had to read at his Bar Mitzvah ceremony – was from the Book of Numbers, *Ba'Midbar,* as it is called in Hebrew. He practiced it with me in his room many times. I noticed how good his Hebrew had gotten. He could read without hesitation, and he pronounced every syllable clearly, with the emphasis in all the right places. I knew he was going to make the Rosen family very proud at his Bar Mitzvah.

On the big day, Davey practiced with me once more, early in the morning, before the family left for the synagogue. Just before he left, he hugged me and said, "You've been my best friend since the day I met you, Shunra!"

I had never thought of it like that, but it made me very glad to know that Davey did.

When he left, I thought of him reciting the opening words of his parsha in front of the whole congregation. I could hear him saying:

"God said to Moses: Make two silver trumpets; of hammered work you shall make them; and you shall use them for summoning the congregation."

It made me proud to think that Davey, like Moses, would be calling the whole congregation to a special meeting, because Davey was like Moses to me – he was my own personal Moses. He had saved me from a terrible fate, something like the misery of the slavery of the Jews in Egypt. And, from that time on, I realized that our friendship was equally special to both of us, which made me even more proud!

The years since Davey's Bar Mitzvah have passed very quickly and Davey is now in his final year of high school. With every college application he fills out, he tells me something about the school, and how it's different from all the other colleges he's applied to. He knows that he wants to study medicine, but he isn't sure if he wants to be a regular doctor or a veterinarian.

I'll never know why Davey and his family are so kind to me, but it doesn't matter. I'll stay with them for the rest of my life, feeling like the happiest of

creatures, blessed, in the special blessing that God has for non-humans. But just as important, I've learned something from living with the Rosen family. Now I know that every creature has a God-given task to perform during his or her lifetime. I thought about it a lot, until I finally realized what mine is. My God-given purpose in life is to help Davey grow into a kind and happy adult – one who believes in himself and knows that he is capable of helping others. And even though I'm only a cat, somehow I know I'll do it!

WHERE'S ARI?

By Devorah Grossman

Devorah
Grossman

Devorah teaches English in elementary school in Jerusalem, Israel. She has a special education background which is put to good use helping disabled children who are part of the synagogue program in her neighborhood.

"Many of us don't have the opportunity to get to know these children on a daily basis. I've tried to show what it is like to have a special child in the home."

Devorah is active in the Jewish Special Needs Forum which is for those who care for children like Ari, the main character of this story. The website for this organization is:
www.geocities.com/jewishgroups

WHERE'S ARI?

What is this? Where's Momma? It's hot. Where's Momma?

Here's Ari's blankie. It's very warm. I'm glad it's warm. Ari likes to be warm. It's warm here, just like when Momma holds me. Maybe even warmer. Silly 'Liza! Where is she now? Look – all the other kids left. Ari didn't leave. Ari is still in bed. Momma and 'Liza and Sarah don't know how warm Ari feels here. Where's Momma?

Oh, my nose! Ari's nose itches. That feels funny. Momma! Ari's nose feels funny. Ari's thirsty. Where's my bottie? Ari's thirsty. Momma! Ari's very thirsty and Ari's nose feels funny.

My head hurts, my eyes hurt, and I'm dizzy. Ari wants to go to sleep. Momma! Momma! Momma! Momma! Momma! Momma!

HEY, WHO'S THE BOSS AROUND HERE?

"OK, everybody, stand back so that we can take a picture of him with all his hair. It's our last chance." Yoni, the photographer, was getting the kids ready. The whole family was gathered together for Ari's third birthday. His hair was going to be cut for the first time.

"Look how long his hair grew!" Momma said. "It's a shame he's not a girl."

"Aliza, help Ari stand up straight. Ari, smile when I say the Hebrew word for cheese, '*Gveena.*'"

"Ari," burst out Aliza. "Would you please stay still for a few seconds? You're driving me nuts!"

Ari's unsteady walk could drive anybody crazy. He has cerebral palsy so he can't use his muscles like other children. He can't stand properly, it's difficult to understand his speech, and he needs help for just about everything he does.

"Gveeena!" called out Yoni. "No, let's try that again. Now all you kids together. I say cheese, oops, Gveena, and everyone smiles. Everyone! How many kids are there?"

"Five plus one," Dina's answer rang out.

"What's this, a math lesson?"

The photographer apparently thought this was a joke, but the rest of the family understood what Dina meant. Five normal kids, and one embarrassing brother with CP who gets all the attention.

"Kids, would you please get out of the way! We don't want to see *you* in this picture. You had your chance when you were his age. We want to see Ari."

"We want to see Ari," mimicked Miri, acting more like Ari than like a twelve-year-old.

"Ari, Ari, Ari," muttered ten-year-old Elan. "That's all we ever hear. It's been three years now!"

Dina nodded in agreement. "Yes, this is the

third birthday of Mr. Attention-Getter. Some people like to lap up all the attention they can possibly get. Tehila and Adi in my class come from Israel. They call it *Tzumi* in hebrew."

"Tzumi? What does that mean?"

"Attention. They said that it's short for *Tzumat lev.*"

"I like that. Tzumi, tzumi, tzumi."

"And we're actually celebrating those three years of tzumi!" Aliza added.

"Dina, would you please move aside?" Yoni was getting more and more frustrated as he tried to get a good close-up of Ari.

Dina sulked and moved aside. *They never care about me. They always forget me. That's because I'm only eight. They don't even notice that I'm here. They don't even look at me. Everybody cares about Ari, Ari, Ari. It's always Ari. It's never Dina.*

Ari's foot jerked forward, and Momma said, "Are you OK, Ari? It's his CP, Yoni."

The children were starving by the time they finally got the formalities out of the way. They had come for the party food, not for Ari's haircut.

Elan plunked himself down by Dad. Little five-year-old Sarah came running over. "No! You always sit by Dad! I want to sit here."

"No. You always sit by Dad. Now it's my turn."

Aliza, who was the eldest in the family, rolled

her eyes at them. "Can't you guys grow up? You're such babies!"

She can also grow up some, thought Miri.

Finally, they were all seated. Aliza and Miri kept bringing out dishes. "Hey, Miri," Dina called out. "That wasn't fair. We all want the dark franks 'n' jackets!" *Miri really should have served the others before taking food for herself,* Dina thought.

"You're not supposed to look in other people's dishes!" Miri retorted.

"Children!" Dad gritted his teeth.

"Not again, please." Momma looked strained.

Grandma looked at her knowingly. She had also been thinking about Miri's Bat Mitzvah which had been a few months earlier. The children's behavior had gotten out of hand, and the adults had been very upset.

Elan had stuck his face into the camera every time Yoni wanted to take a picture. Aliza didn't want to be in any pictures.

"As long as Ari is in the picture," wailed Sarah, "I don't want to be part of it."

Of course, Dina didn't want to give in either.

So the picture was a mess, the meal was a mess, the whole evening was a mess, and everybody was getting angry, dirty and exhausted.

And it looked as if it would happen again tonight.

"Oops," Dina gasped to Miri. "I didn't mean

to push over the juice. I just wanted to get to my seat." *It's about time I learned to accept it,* Dina thought, her teeth clenched. *I'm a born klutz.*

"Momma, tell Dina to leave me alone. She's bothering me again. Tell her to sit over there."

"Now look at what you did!" Aliza called out in shock to Elan. He barely even noticed. "My new blouse is all red from the beets."

"Kids, will you please sit quietly?" Momma pleaded. "Everybody's looking at you."

"Momma!" That was Sarah. "Elan's touching my plate. Now it has his germs all over it. I need a new plate. I can't eat from his germs!"

I can't understand where she gets all her crazy ideas, Dina thought. *I didn't know germs existed until she started talking about them. And she's only five! She's always coming up with brilliant ideas. She likes to read books that others her age would never pick up. Stars. China. Ships. Medicine. She knows all about Ari's CP from her books. She understands what Janet, the physiotherapist, said – that he would walk in a few months. She herself wants to be a physiotherapist, so that she can help children learn how to use their muscles, how to eat on their own, how to stand, and how to walk. What a crazy kid!*

"It's not germs," said Elan. "You're a germ. My hands are clean. Momma made me take a bath

this morning."

"Elan, you just got the top layer off."

"Sarah, that's disgusting," Aliza said.

"So are his hands."

"Mo-o-omma!" It was Elan this time. "Will you take her away from me! She's bo-o-othering me. Make her sit at the other end of the table with the old people like you."

It was then that Elan and Aliza noticed that Grandma was staring at them. Grandma mumbled something to Granddad about "Today's Kids," and then made believe that she didn't notice them any more.

Granddad tried to ignore them, and stared at the broken flowerpot at the other end of the table. How did that happen? The flower had been kicked out of the pot and it landed some distance away. Too bad – it had been watered recently. Well, actually it wasn't water. It was juice.

"Elan," warned Dad. "Don't you dare."

It was too late. Elan had already removed the cover from the salt shaker and poured its contents into Ari's fruit salad.

"Selma," Aunt Debbie said, to divert everyone's attention. "The salmon is great. What did you put into this, curry?"

"Bernie, is your Rivkie graduating this year?"

"How's your art work, Arthur? Did you ever finish that painting?

"Shimon, whatever hap-
pened to the computer course
you were supposed to teach?"

Uncle Shimon looked away
while responding. He didn't want to watch while his
niece, Sarah, sampled everybody's drinks.

The evening couldn't end fast enough.

The King of the Evening got his hair cut. More
importantly, he got his attention even though he certainly didn't deserve it.

Tzumi, again.

What About Me?

The next morning the kids got up as usual and
heard Momma scurrying about.

"Good morning, children. Get up quickly.
You'll be leaving for school fifteen minutes early so
that I can take Ari to Dr. Freed. Hurry up. Come on,
Sarah. Elan, let's go. Miri, here's your school uni-
form. Yes, I know that it's a bit wrinkled. I didn't get
a chance to iron it last night because Ari couldn't
sleep all night. I'll try to get to it tonight if I can."

Even with her sleepy brain, Miri managed to
think, *Boy, how helpful. Now I need an ironed shirt;
tonight I get it. And all 'cuz of that beloved Ari.*

Ari took away a lot of his parents' time. They
didn't have much to spare for the other children. At
least one parent had to take him to doctors and thera-
pists so that he could learn how to use his muscles.

The other kids were often left alone at home.

"Aliza, did you brush your teeth?"

"Arrghuxitungg."

"I didn't hear you – would you please repeat that?"

"Arrghuxitungg!"

"Momma, is this my lunch?" asked Elan. "Hey, Miri, give it back to me right now."

"I got a torn sammidge bag."

"Say 'sandwich' and I'll give you a good bag."

"Sammidge."

"Ari," Elan turned to him, a sly look on his face. "Say 'sandwich.' Can you say it? Can you say it?"

"Ah-idge. Ah-idge."

Elan reached into his pocket and removed an unidentified, shapeless, and gooey glob. "If you say it again, I'll give you the caramel that Yoel gave me yesterday." He rolled it merrily between his hands.

Ari wanted the sweet candy very much. Even more, he desperately wanted some friendly contact with his older brother.

"Ah-idge."

"Amazing. What three-year old can't say 'sand-wich?'"

Elan was about to hand his caramel over to Ari, when he thought of a better idea. He dipped the caramel into the salt shaker from the dining room table, and then handed it over to his brother. Ari, with a bit of difficulty, got it into his mouth. His con-

torted face showed that he didn't know whether it was sweet or salty.

Elan and the little kids burst out laughing.

"You're such babies," said Aliza, but she did not remove the candy from Ari's mouth.

"Kids," called Momma from the girls' bedroom, "Get dressed quickly. Come, Sarah, Momma will dress you."

"Momma – your hands are cold."

"Then let's get dressed fast."

The children finally got out of the house, ten minutes late. They did not exchange any friendly words until they arrived at school.

"Bye, Sarah, have a nice day in kindergarten," called Aliza.

"Bye, Elan. Bye, Dina and Miri. Have a nice day."

Elan was finding it hard to concentrate in class.

"...which is why Yaacov stayed for another seven years. A week after marrying Leah, he...."

"Psst, Dov," Elan whispered to the boy in front of him. "Did you finish your math homework?"

"Yes, and you're not getting it this time. I worked hard on it last night with my dad."

"C'mon, one last time."

"No, it's not fair."

"Dov, is anything the matter?" It was Rabbi Brodkin.

"No."

"Were you talking again?"

"But, Rabbi Brodkin, Elan called me. He started talking, not me."

"Elan again? What did we say last time you disturbed other kids?"

"Dunno."

"Oh, yes you do."

"You're always blaming me. You never say anything to anybody else."

"Elan!" Rabbi Brodkin said sharply. *Uh, oh*, thought almost every boy in class. Kids just didn't talk back to Rabbi Brodkin.

"Sure, go ahead," he ranted. "What else can you pile on me? Maybe I cheated on a test. Maybe I came late to class. Maybe I put a frog on your chair. Huh? What else?"

"Elan, kindly go to the office. Do not come back to class unless you have a written note from the principal."

Elan left the class and trudged down to the big, brown office.

"Yes? Can I help you, Elan?" said Rabbi Goodman looking up from his work.

"Rabbi Brodkin sent me."

Rabbi Goodman listened to the story from Elan's point of view, and said, "Look, Elan. You're being sent to me too frequently. I'm warning you: if I hear one more complaint about you, I will have no choice but to suspend you from school for an entire day. I do not recommend that. Now go back to class with this note for your teacher, and I hope I don't see you again in this office. Ever. Have a nice day."

Back in class, Elan couldn't wait for the period to be over. Everybody was staring at him. What a horrible day!

Brrrring!

Elan gathered his things together. *Finally! I thought this period would never end.* As he got up to leave, he felt a sharp sting on his cheek. "Ouch! Who shot that rubber band at me?"

He spun around and pointed a finger at Baruch, who was staring intently at the ceiling with a guilty look on his face. "I'm gonna get you!" Adrenaline surging, he charged over and punched him in the jaw. "That'll fix you!"

Baruch wasn't about to be outdone. He kicked Elan's leg. "Now you'll hobble like your baby brother." He paraded clumsily around the room, making believe he was losing his balance. Elan grabbed Baruch by the neck and shook him. "And this is for your stupid sister!" he yelled.

The principal, Rabbi Goodman, passed by just at that moment. "Elan! What are you doing? Fighting? In *my* school? Come into my office this very instant!"

With a defiant look on his face, Elan followed Rabbi Goodman to the office.

Ah, here we go again. I think I know every nook and cranny of this ugly old office. How do you like that – twice in one day. What will he do to me now? Who cares! So he'll send me home. There I'm not teased about my brother. At least I gave it to Baruch. He deserved it. Weird, isn't it, that I stuck up for Ari. True, he gets all the tzumi in the family. But I won't let anybody make fun of him. Hey, it's not his fault he can't walk, is it?

"Elan Rosenfeld!" He was brought back to the present. "How many times have you been in this office since Hanukkah? You have great potential, and you can perform superbly, but you consistently engage in degrading, undignified, and mischievous actions. How dare you lay your hands on another pupil? And less than half an hour after exiting my office.

"You were informed of the consequences. I regret that you will have to be suspended for an entire day. A note to that effect will be placed in your permanent record. Your mother will be told, and she will pick you up. Sit quietly in that chair until she arrives."

Two hours later, back at home, Momma sat him down.

"I know that it's difficult for you, Elan," she began. "It's difficult for all of us. Ari is a special boy who needs a lot of attention."

Right, thought Elan cynically. *And we don't.*

"When we discovered Ari's CP, we were very worried about you kids. We didn't know how you would manage with a special child in the family. We didn't even know how we, Dad and I, would be able to take care of him and the rest of you. Would Ari manage in a house full of active, fun-loving kids? We knew that he would take away a lot of the attention that would have been given to our other children."

"I hardly even remember the time before he was born."

"Yes, he kind of took over our lives."

"Nobody here thinks about anything but Ari's appointments, his meals, and his phyosi – physoi – phosi – "

"Physiotherapy. I know. And you also want to have fun together, right?"

"Right. I mean, we're your kids, too."

"And we love you all very much, and we only want the best for you."

"Not only Ari's best."

"Of course not, Elan! We want the best for all of our children. We like to have special times with

61

every child. As a matter of fact, you know what, let's do something fun today. Right now. I know you were punished for doing something really bad in school. We taught you kids never to hit another human being."

"Yeah," Elan lapsed into lecture mode. "If we have something to handle with someone, no matter what he did, we should first talk to an adult."

"It's simply that a teacher, parent, or older friend may see things differently, and may be able to offer some wise advice. But anyway, let's make ourselves a super-duper Momma-type pizza, just the two of us, with juice and ice cream. Ari and the girls won't be home from day care and school for another two hours. How does that sound?"

"Just us? That sounds super-duper Momma-type amazing!" exclaimed Elan excitedly.

Once they sat down, Momma told stories about when she was a little girl.

"I would get up at 6:00 each morning, so that I could walk half an hour to the 6:59 train. After a 25-minute ride, I transferred to a different train, and then to a bus – all in order to study in a Jewish school...."

"And I hardly manage to get up and dressed in the morning!" said Elan.

Two hours later, though it seemed like ten minutes, his sisters came home from school, pushing Ari in his wheel chair. They left him in the living room.

Interrupting each other, they didn't even notice that their excited chatter had broken a peaceful calm at home.

"My teacher returned our tests, and I got a 94 in Math."

"…so she allowed me to pet the rabbit during the break."

"There was so much blood when she fell down, and then they bandaged her knee. It was so ugly that I could hardly look at her. Two teeth fell out."

"…and she yelled at her for no reason, and it wasn't her fault."

"…so I have to interview three people and announce the results to my class."

Suddenly, Miri noticed Elan standing quietly by the wall. "Hey, Elan, what are you doing here? You're not supposed to come home until 5:00."

"I'm home," he replied.

"Coulda fooled me," she answered sarcastically.

"Momma," Aliza tactfully changed the subject. "I have a test on Hebrew verbs tomorrow. Yicch – I don't know nothing, *klum!* Can you please help me, Momma?"

"When I come home from Ari's doctor," Momma replied. "I hope to help you for a few minutes. Aliza, you're thirteen. You'll just have to take your schoolwork more seriously – I can't spend so much time with you when Ari demands so much of us."

"But *Momma*," Aliza started. *There's that tzumi again. Ari needs his attention.*

Momma silenced her with a warning look, and turned to Miri.

"Did you finish your science paper?"

"No, Momma, I asked you to help me find some clip art so that I can…."

"Right. I couldn't do it yesterday, as you know. How did the family tree go? Did you hand it in today?"

"Yes, but my teacher said it wasn't very nice. I don't care."

"Show me please."

"Here."

Momma look at the picture Miri handed her. The teacher was right. It really wasn't nice. Every family member was an apple – Dad and his family, Momma and her family, and the kids. Way down near the ground was a rotten apple with a worm peeking out. On it was written *Ari*.

"Miriam!" Momma really looked hurt now. Using Miri's full name proved it.

"Can Shani come over tomorrow to study with me?" interrupted Dina.

"No, honey, not tomorrow. The physical therapist is coming for Ari. I can't have kids running around then."

"But *Momma*…."

"Momma," Sarah chimed in. "My teacher said

that every time I do a good thing, you need to sign this page. Am I good, Momma?"

"Come, sweetheart. Show me the page. After you help me clean up from supper, I'll have some time to sign. OK?"

Brrrring!

"Dina, get the phone, please!"

"Hello?"

"Hello. Can I speak to Elan? This is Baruch."

"Just a sec. Elan! Baruch wants to talk to you."

Baruch? Thought Elan. *What does he want from me? Didn't he make enough trouble at school today?*

"Hi, Baruch," said Elan.

"Hi Elan," Baruch said, breathlessly. "My mommy told me to call and made me say I'm sorry, and she's standing next to me right now, so I'm sorry, and that's all. Are you still coming over like we decided?"

"Well...."

"Hey, c'mon, we're still friends, aren't we? It was just something I said, and you know I didn't mean to insult you, and you know I have the same problem."

"It was still pretty nasty to say."

"Right. I said I'm sorry. I'll watch my mouth in the future. Now are you coming over?"

Pause. "When did we say I'm coming?"

"5:30. Fine. Thanks. See ya soon."

Baruch's sister, who had Down Syndrome, greeted Elan at the door.

"Hi. Bawuk, heeuh is Elan," she pointed.

"Thank you, Becky. Elan, I'll just finish reading her this story, and then we'll go into my room."

A few minutes later, while they were playing, Becky wandered in.

"Becky, do you want to join us? We're playing Save the Dolphin. You be the dolphin, and we'll save you from the fishermen."

"Me dolbin."

Elan was amazed at how much fun they were having saving Becky the "dolbin."

"Boys, do you want something to eat?" asked Baruch's mother, coming in to the room. "It's almost seven."

"Seven?" Elan echoed. "I have to be back home by 7:45."

"Didn't think it was so late," said Baruch.

"Didn't think we could play with your little sister, and still have such a good time."

"She *is* a lot of fun. Let's go sit down. We'll eat quickly."

At the table, Elan was shocked to see the contrast between this family and his own.

"Tova, you sat by Becky yesterday. Now it's my turn to help her."

"But yesterday she was able to eat almost by

herself. I hardly did anything."
She made a long face, then
added, "But OK. It's your turn."

*Fighting to feed a special
child?* thought Elan incredulously. *What a family!
They play with her and tell her stories, even though
she takes up hours of their time.*

Back at home, Miri was telling everyone about
her field trip to a school for children with CP. Elan
walked in just in time. "Our teacher wants us to
volunteer there once a week."

"Once a week?" exclaimed Aliza. "Tell her that
she should volunteer in *our* house."

"But it was really nice there. They help the
children learn how to manage in life. They've made
a lot of progress with some of the children."

"How can a child who can barely move do anything? What kind of progress are you talking about?"
Dina asked. "I don't see any progress in Ari. He still
walks like a little baby."

"They say that it takes time. They'll show us
how to help these kids."

"So you'll learn how to help Ari."

"Ha, ha. Maybe Ari will learn how to help me."

"Anyway, we'll be going there again next week,
and then we'll go every Monday."

"How old are the kids there?"

"Six to thirteen years old. Why?"

"I was just wondering whether we could send Ari to that school."

"Send Ari to a school for dummies?"

"Not dummies." Miri tried to be patient. "These children can't use their muscles like we can, but that doesn't mean that all of them are dumb."

"That's right. Ari isn't dumb. But he needs a school for children like him."

"And if he stays there," Dina brought them back to her train of thought, "then it'll be better for us at home."

"Yeah!"

"Ari won't take our Dad and Momma away from us all the time. He will have others to take care of him."

"People like Miri."

"That's pretty selfish of us, isn't it? I mean, Ari is part of the family...."

"And we're also part of the family. A big part. We also deserve a Dad and a Momma."

"Who cares? He's only three now. We'd still have three more long years to suffer with him."

"Do you really think that Dad and Momma will send him to a special school?"

"I doubt it."

"Of course they wouldn't. He's their little child. But it's always nice to imagine."

"What if Ari were never born in the first place?"

"Come on, this is ridiculous."

"Fine. I'm tired."

"And I still have some studying left. Bye, guys."

Miri couldn't sleep that night. She heard her parents talking softly in their room.

"I don't know what else to do," Momma was saying.

"I know what you mean," Dad responded. "I've asked them so many times to be more understanding. All they do is pull more pranks on the poor kid. I told you what Elan did to his fruit salad when Ari got his hair cut."

"Dr. Hersh, the psychologist, said that the kids should also help to take care of Ari. That way they'll feel that he is part of the family, rather than just a burden sapping our strength."

"But they refuse to have anything to do with him."

"They won't even take him on a walk. They don't want to be seen with him."

"It's a big deal for them to take him to and from day care."

"As time goes on, and with the new baby on the way, I find it more and more difficult to scoop him up from the floor each time he needs to be picked

up. The kids should be doing that."

"Did you ever speak to Dave Abram's uncle about it? I hear he's a very good child therapist."

"Yes, I did. I've been thinking that perhaps we should make an appointment with him and get some help. I want to be sure we're doing the right thing."

"The right thing about what?"

"I was thinking… no. You'll never agree to this."

"What?"

"Forget it. You're a mother. No mother would ever agree to my idea."

"Well…?"

"I really don't see any other way."

"Please don't talk to me in riddles."

"What I was thinking was, perhaps we should put him in a school for children like him. I heard of a very good one in Atlanta, Georgia."

"Georgia? But that's so far away! He'd have to dorm there."

"I know."

"He's our son!"

"And we have another son and four daughters to think about too."

"He's so young. He just turned three!"

"Right. And we have another child on the way."

"It's cruel to do such a thing to him."

"I didn't think you'd like the idea."

"I don't. But you may be right. Our other

children need our attention, too."

At this, tears began to well up in Miri's eyes. *So they do understand how we feel. But aren't we causing a terrible thing to happen? Sending Ari away....*

"What do we explain to the kids?" Momma wondered.

"They would probably take it just fine. How do we explain this to Ari? He may have trouble moving around a bit, but he sure is bright!"

"If only he could express himself...."

"And in spite of it all, he's still such a major part of the family," Dad said.

"Yes. How can we even think of doing this to him?"

Dads face turned stern. "Look, you see what's happening to the other kids. Take Elan. He never had trouble in school. Aliza was always at the top in her class. Dina never hurt a fly. How else can we deal with this?"

Yes, yes! Miri wanted to shout. Go do it. But she didn't dare. She heard Dad getting up and Momma sniffling. She dashed back into bed, crashing into Aliza's bed along the way.

"Hey, lea' me alone!" Aliza said.

"Aliza, you just don't understand. Dad and Momma are sending Ari to school in Georgia. Soon we'll have our parents back, like before he was born."

"What? Why are they doing that? Lea' me alone." And with that she was back in slumber-land.

The next day, Aliza got a call at school. It was Dad.

"Aliza, I'm at the hospital with Momma."

"Wow, Dad. When did you go? Momma was fine when we left for school. Yay, Dad!"

"I'm sure you'll handle things well while we're gone. Please bring all the kids home from school as usual. Take care of them, and give everyone supper and a bath. Don't forget that my cell phone number is on the fridge."

"If I need anything, I can ask the neighbors, right?"

"Yeah, but try not to bother them too much."

"Fine. Dad, you'll call when there's news, right? Right away!"

"Of course, honey. Look, Momma needs me now. Be in touch and take care of everything. OK?"

"Sure, Dad. Send Momma our love and tell us when it happens."

"OK. Bye, Aliza."

"Bye."

"What happened, Aliza?" Naomi, the school secretary, asked.

"My momma, she's in the hospital – "

"In the hospital?" asked Mrs. Skwerut, the math teacher.

"Don't worry, she's OK. She's going to have a

baby."

"Well, congratulations!"

"Thank you. I didn't know it would happen so soon. And this morning she didn't tell us anything. Ooooh! I wonder what it'll be."

"That's wonderful, Aliza."

"How's you're mother doing?"

"Dad said she was fine. I'm running to tell my friends."

Is it 911 or 102?

"Mazal Tov! You have a new baby boy."

"Is he healthy?"

"He's fine."

"Are you sure? We have a child with CP in our family."

"Yes, we checked for that too. He seems to be in perfect shape. CP is usually discovered later on, but from what we can see, he's doing great. No need to worry."

"Thank you." Turning his face upward, he added, "And thank You, God."

The excited children visited Momma that evening.

"Oh, he's so cute."

"Can I hold him?"

"Now we're six plus one," Dina whispered to Sarah. Unfortunately, Momma heard, and gave her a look of mixed sadness and anger.

"When is the *Brit*?"

"If he was born Monday, then it's probably next Monday."

"What do you think they'll name him?"

"We're not supposed to talk about it before-hand."

"Too bad. I'm so curious."

On Monday, at the brit – the circumcision – the new baby was named Daniel, or Danny for short.

"I hope this time I have a normal brother to play with," Elan whispered to Miri.

"Yeah, even if you're ten years older than him."

"I don't care how old he is, as long as he can move his arms and legs."

They both looked in the direction of Ari.

Late Monday night, Aliza and Miri eaves-dropped on their parents' whispered conversation.

"What are they saying, Aliza?" she asked.

"Shhh. Let's go over to the door. Dad and Momma are talking about Ari and us. Did you know they want to put him in a school far away from home?"

Miri nodded.

"How did you know? Shhh. Listen."

"I spoke to Dave Abram's uncle." Dad was say-ing. "He suggested a few more institutions. Happy Days in Miami is for kids from five to fourteen. We still might be able to get Ari in if we're lucky. And if

74

not this place – "

"Don't you think we can somehow manage without sending away our baby?"

"You know we can't go on like this any more."

"But Ari isn't as bad off as some of the other kids. Some children with CP are also brain-damaged. Some really can't move and they have twisted arms and fingers. Ari isn't like that. We just have to work it out somehow with the other kids."

"How much longer should we try to 'work it out with the other kids'? How many years should the rest of our children suffer?"

"I guess you're right again. Oh, my baby…."

"Anyway, I had also been looking into institutions in New York and Boston, Massachusetts."

"Jewish?"

"Some yes, some no. But they're good places. As far as I can see, the best one is in Boston. They help brighter children like our Ari improve so that they can be mainstreamed in regular schools."

"Mainstreamed?"

"Yes, put into regular schools, so that they can learn with normal kids."

"That sounds nice. I assume that will take a while. During that time, maybe the kids will grow up enough to accept him better."

"Having Baby Danny around will definitely help."

75

"Yes. OK. I'll go check on the baby. Tomorrow is Election Day. You're off from work. Will you be able to check out that place in Boston?"

"That sounds like a good idea. I'll leave first thing in the morning. Rachel, just remember, it's all for the best."

"Yes, it is. We have to remember that. Thanks."

"Good night."

Aliza and Miri flew back into bed.

It's really gonna happen, thought Miri. *They're sending him away.*

"It's a shame, though, isn't it?" Aliza whispered thoughtfully. "I mean, he's really a little baby."

"So?" Asked Miri. "He'll have big people taking care of him there, and we will finally have a Dad and a Momma, too."

"Still...."

"Let's go back to sleep. I'm tired."

"I'm still not sure this is the right thing to do."

"Don't worry. I'm sure it is. You remember what Dad said. How much longer can the rest of us suffer?"

How selfish of us, thought Aliza. She did not share her feelings with Miri.

"Anyway, let's go back to sleep. Tomorrow we're home from school. I don't want to be tired then. Good night, Miri."

"Good night."

The little ones started to wake up just as Momma was giving Aliza last-minute instructions for lunch.

"Just cut up a vegetable salad and then peel and dice the carrots and potatoes. We'll do the actual cooking when I get back, at around one. I don't want you to use the stove when I'm not home."

"Momma, I'm thirteen."

"Right. And I want you to be fourteen, and fifteen, and sixteen, till 120, Amen. The potato peeler is in the milchig drawer. You can ask the others to help, too."

"No prob."

"I put Ari in his crib by the kitchen window, so that you can keep an eye on him while you get the food ready. If he needs anything, I'm sure you'll be able to help him."

It's a good thing you're sure, 'cuz I'm not, she thought.

"I gave him a cup of milk. He might need help so he doesn't spill it all over the crib."

"OK, Momma. We'll take care of everything. We're big."

"You'll be OK? I'll be in touch. Just make sure the kids stay out of trouble. I'm not used to leaving you by yourselves for so many hours, but today there's really no choice. I'm taking Danny to the doctor and

then I'm going to vote."

"Don't worry, Momma. We'll be good."

"Fine. Call if you need me. Bye, dear."

After breakfast, Dina and Sarah went into their bedroom at the far end of the house to bake their own special "cake." They also wanted to be out of earshot, so that Aliza wouldn't get angry.

"Put the cocoa in this cup."

Sarah poured in some dirt from the back yard. Dina added sugar and chocolate chips.

"Should I get water?"

"Yes," Dina whispered back. "But only from the guest bathroom right here. The other bathroom is too close to the kitchen and living room, where the big kids are."

"Fine. I'll go to this bathroom."

"Here," Sarah called, as she closed the bedroom door behind her. "Is this enough?"

"Yes. Now wait here while I get the 'oven.'"

"I know Dad and Momma have candles and matches in their bedroom…"

"No, we're not allowed in there."

"Then I'll have to go into the kitchen. I hope Aliza doesn't see me."

Dina went into the kitchen and took two candles and a box of matches. Aliza didn't even notice her.

"Here," she said as soon as she came back. "Hold the candle, while I strike the match."

"One, two, three, go!"

It took a few tries, but they finally got the candles lit.

"Now, while you hold the candles, I'll hold the cup with the cake."

"Dina, I don't feel like holding these candles."

"So put them on the floor."

"But that's too close to the bed. If we put it there – "

"Ow! Some wax dripped onto my pinkie!"

"Show me. Where is the candle?"

"Dunno. Maybe it fell. Look here, it hurts. Ow, ouch. I need cold water."

"Here, there is some water left in the cup."

"I'll ask Aliza – "

"SARAH! Look! The bed!"

"AI-I-I!"

"It's getting bigger. Look at the pillow."

"Dina, this is *fire!* It's getting bigger. Aliza!!"

"Aliza! Come here! Help!"

"What's the matter?" Aliza called from the kitchen.

"Fire!"

Aliza came dashing in. "What happened? Where are – Oh, no, no! Come here. Now. We gotta get out of here, fast!"

By now almost the whole bed was in flames. The laundry hamper also caught fire.

"Elan! Miri! Come here!"

Together they tried to put out the fire by beating it with a towel.

"I'm getting the water," shouted Elan. He made the fire hiss and sizzle, but he didn't accomplish very much.

"Let's get more buckets," shouted Miri. Soon everyone was running back and forth with cups and bottles and buckets and pots.

By now the fire had made its way to the boys' bedroom to their left and to the older girls' bedroom a little further away. The fire was crackling and lapping its tongues as it closed in around them at them. It was inching its way along the thick red and black carpeting. They had just moments to decide where to go.

"We just have to get out of here right *now*," Aliza screamed. Miri spun around and pointed to the front door at the other end of the living room.

"We can't go there. It's blocked by fire. We're going to die! Die! We'll all be dead. We're going to burn up right here, Aliza."

"No, we won't. Everybody dash – now – into the parents' bedroom. Dina, what are you waiting for? Run!"

"We can't go into that bedroom," Dina said. "We're not allowed in there."

"Then blame me. Now move!" yelled Aliza above the crackling noises. "The house is on fire. Do you understand? On FIRE!"

Elan climbed up and out the second-floor window, and then jumped down. Realizing that he'd left all his siblings behind, he called out,

"See how I did it? Now you do it just like me."

"The higher is getting fire! I mean, the fire is getting higher. I mean, get me out of here. Help. Help. Help," yelled Miri. She grabbed a pillow and jumped out the window.

"Ow! My arm! My arm!"

Elan went over to her. "We'll check your arm later."

"Elan, catch her!" Aliza was in the bedroom window, holding Sarah.

It was a beautiful catch. Any basketball player would have been jealous.

"It's your turn, Dina."

"I'm scared, Aliza. It's high."

"No, it's not. Just jump. I'll push you."

She held her – screaming and kicking – and just barely managed to get her to the window.

"No!!" Dina shrieked. "No! Help! Momma! Aliiiiza!"

"Elan," Aliza called down. "Catch her! Dina, aim for Elan's hands."

Thud! Before Dina knew what was happening, she fell through Elan's arms and onto the grass.

It was Aliza's turn. She was the only one at

the window now. Now *she* got cramps in her stomach.

"Miri, I'm scared. What do I do?"

"Aliza, don't think about it. Just jump!"

"It's so high!"

"Jump, Aliza, jump!"

"The fire!" Aliza saw how big it was. It was already creeping into the parents' bedroom. It could burn her up any minute now... "It's huge."

"Come on Aliza, it's just a teensy jump."

"Don't look, just jump."

"Turn around and jump backwards," yelled Elan. "It's easier that way."

Aliza glanced back inside the house, gasped, and jumped.

Once on the ground, Aliza said, "Where's a phone?"

"There's one by the newspaper stand down the block," said Miri.

"That's much too far."

"Let's just run next door and ask Mrs. Benjamin."

Everybody but Miri ran over and knocked on Mrs. Benjamin's door.

"Why doesn't she answer the door already?"

"Maybe they're not at home," said Aliza. "Let's go to somebody else."

Miri saw a stranger across the street. He was leaning on a tree, talking on a cell phone. *I gotta call*

the fire department! She wanted to say. *Give me your phone now!*

She caught herself before uttering the words, and realized, *he's a stranger*.

Meanwhile, Elan ran down the block. Tzvi was up in his treehouse.

"Tzvi! Help! Fire! Call the fire! My house! Run to the fire department! Tzvi, See! Fire! Big. Big fire! In *my* house!"

Tzvi shinnied down and dashed in to his house. On the way, he shouted over his shoulder, "911 or 102? What do I dial? I forgot!"

Back outside, he announced, "The firemen are shinnying down the pole right now. Remember how I shinnied down the tree? I'd make a great fireman, wouldn't I?"

He thought this was all one big game. A joke.

Elan and Tzvi rushed back to the house, where the others were watching the fire helplessly.

"Look at those flames! They're coming out of the door!"

"Wow! Did you hear that? That was the bedroom window!"

"Oh my goodness. It just popped."

"That's the window we just jumped from!"

"The new curtains Momma made. Dad loved them so much."

"Look, the living room is starting to burn."

"The kitchen and bathroom are next."

"That means our whole house will be destroyed."

"The windows are so black."

"And so hot."

"Dollya!" Sarah cried. "I forgot to save her."

"Come on, Sarah. It's just a doll. At least *you* got out!"

"Yeah, but Dollya – she's gonna die!"

"Sarah, we left everything back there. Our schoolbags, books, dishes, furniture, wallets, clothes, towels, everything is there. But at least we got out. We're alive!"

Tzvi's mother rushed to the scene, looked around, and asked, "Where's Ari?"

"Where's Ari?" echoed Aliza.

What is this? Where's Momma? It's hot. Where's Momma?

Here's Ari. I am Ari. Here's blankie. It's very warm. I'm glad it's warm. Ari likes to be warm. It's warm here, just like when Momma holds Ari. Momma holds me. Maybe even warmer. Silly 'Liza! Where is she now? Look – all the other kids left. Ari didn't leave. Ari is still here in bed. Momma and 'Liza and Sarah don't know how warm Ari feels here. Where's Momma?

"Where's Ari?" Miri panicked. "We gotta save him! We *must* save him! Poor Ari! Poor Ari! Oy – he'll die! He'll die! We *have* to save him. Poor Ari."

Dina told her, "The fire-men are coming. They'll save him."

"No, they're not here now. By the time they come he could be – he could be – he could be...."

"Miri, for once, please be quiet. We have to do something. I'm tall enough to reach the window. I'll go in and get him."

"You can't go in, Aliza. The whole place is on fire. We gotta help Ari. We can't. We gotta. How can we go in? We gotta save him."

"And I was worried about Dollya."

"And I said that we *all* got out and that we're all alive...."

Meanwhile, Elan was going around the house trying to find a place to climb in.

The flames are all over! How can I get in?

The kitchen window. Ari's in the kitchen.

He started to shinny up the water spout by the kitchen window.

"No, no, no, Elan," Miri called to him. "Don't go in!"

"I can't just stand here."

"You'll burn like Ari. Don't go!"

"Go away. He's my brother and I have to save him."

He shoved Miri out of the way, jumped up, grabbed the ledge, and tried to push the window open.

It wouldn't budge.

"I think it's locked."

"Can you break the window?"

"Nope. There's too much pressure from the fire."

Elan dropped down. "Where else?"

"The bathroom window."

"Yeah."

Oh, my nose! Ari's nose itches. That feels funny. Momma! Ari's nose feels funny. Ari's thirsty. Where's my bottie? Ari's thirsty. Momma! Ari's very thirsty and Ari's nose feels funny.

Elan made a leap toward the high window.

"Ow!" He slipped down from the wall, scraping his knee and cutting his hand.

"Maybe I'll stand on the bicycle."

The bicycle seemed to have a mind of its own. Elan crashed to the ground.

"Mo-mma, I wa' Mo-mma," a feeble voice cried out.

"Forget the bicycle. Put your foot here." Using both her hands and all her strength, Aliza tried to heave him upward.

They both fell down.

"Mo-mma, Ari 'ot."

Aliza said, "But there's no other way to get up there. Hold your hands together, and I'll climb up."

'But I... OK." This was no time for arguments.

Aliza climbed up.

I never realized how small this window is.

She snaked her way onto the sink, then jumped down to the floor.

Ow, that hurts. I can hardly breathe! I can't see anything through this smoke.

Ari! I must find him. Where did we leave him? We treated him so badly. I can't even remember where we left him.

Gotta get air.

It dark. Ari wanna sleep.

Aliza jumped up onto the sink under the window, and gulped in some air.

My head hurts. And my eyes. I'm dizzy. Ari wants to go to sleep. Momma! Momma! Momma! Momma! Momma! Momma!

Gotta get Ari.

She stubbed her toe on the bathtub as she ran back.

Gotta get Ari and air, air and Ari.

She realized the grim situation. *Ari needs air. Ari needs out. The kitchen. In his crib. Where's the kitchen? Why doesn't he cry, so I know where to go?*

"C'mon, Ari. Where are you? Aliza's comin'!"

Maybe he can't cry anymore. Do you think he... No. It can't be. He just fell asleep or something.

Back outside, Elan was looking for another window. *It looks like the fire spread to the kitchen.*

In the meantime, Aliza was running toward the kitchen. *Phew, it's so black and smoky!*

"Ari! I'm coming."

Here, I think I'm in the kitchen now.

"Ow! That was hot. I better be careful." Her right hand instinctively slapped the other arm to put out the small flames on her sleeve.

"My arm – burned!" *She sucked in her breath.* "And now I think I burned my hand." *How will I carry Ari out of here? Hey – is he burning too?*

"Ari, Baby, I'm coming!"

Sarah and Dina were crying outside.

"Dad said we're not allowed to use matches. It's dangerous."

"It really is."

"But we were trying to help Momma. We were baking a cake for Shabbat."

"Yes, but Dad said that we're supposed to help with the right things. Like Ari."

"This wasn't help. Ari... Ari...."

Miri was looking at the bathroom window and crying. Her arm was hanging motionless.

Inside, Aliza was desperately trying to find her way into the smoke-filled kitchen.

"Aliza! Are you OK?" She heard Elan yelling.

He too, had been trying to make his way into the house.

Aliza tried the bathroom window but she's still not out. I'll try the kitchen.

As he was climbing up a nearby tree, a burning window popped out and crashed onto his face. Shards of blackened glass seared his skin.

He dropped down. "My hands. I'm burned!"

"Aliza, come out already! Where are you?" Miri was crying.

Dina and Sarah were moaning, "Aliza, Ari, Aliza, Ari...."

"Ari," begged Aliza, "please be OK. We love you Ari."

Maybe I can try to breathe through my sleeve.

Ouch. That must have been the stove. That means the window is here. Then this is his crib.

"Ari! Come here."

She blindly felt around for him.

"Ari, where are you? Ari, dear. Come on."

The fire! It'll reach the kitchen soon, and then there'll be no way to get out of –

"There you are," she found the motionless child.

"Come. Come to Aliza." She picked him up, wet blanket and all.

Sleeping through this? Unbelievable! Is he asleep? Maybe he's really....

"Stop thinking," she told herself out loud.

"Concentrate on getting out of here. Don't look at the bedrooms. Don't look at the fire. Go straight to the bathroom." He brushed against her burned arm as she was picking him up. "Oooh."

Ari whimpered lightly.

"Good, Ari, you woke up."

"A-eeza, me 'ot!"

"Yes, Ari. I'm hot too."

"'ot too."

Maybe now I can go out the front door. No, I can't. The living room is on fire. Back to the bathroom. It's so hot here. I can barely breathe.

As she passed by the stove, she turned off the gas switch. *Just in case,* she thought.

"Ari, please stay alive. We really love you. We'll be good to you. We'll take care of you. Just please live and be healthy. Ari...."

"Me Ari."

"Just live through this fire."

"Fi-uh?"

She looked out the open bathroom window.

"Miri! Catch him!"

"I can't! My arm. Elan! Aliza, don't throw him. He'll fall."

"Throw down the blanket," advised Sarah. "We'll all hold it, and you drop him."

Each child took a corner of the blanket.

Ignoring the burning pain, Elan grabbed a corner with both hands.

"Hold tight. He's heavier than you think."

Thud! Ari looked around and wailed.

"Ari! Ari! You're alive."

"I wanna hold him."

"Me too."

"Aliza," called Elan. He remembered that his sister was still in the burning house. "Climb out the window, hang from your hands, and jump."

"OK." *My head feels like it's floating.* She landed on her ankle. "Ouch! My leg."

Tzvi's mother and Miri helped Aliza hop over to a bench on the sidewalk.

"Thank God. You're such a brave girl, Aliza. Good for you. You saved your brother!"

By now Aliza was exhausted. She collapsed and sobbed on Miri's shoulder.

Dina brought Ari over, and sat with the others on the bench.

The fire trucks finally arrived.

"I've never seen such a massive fire."

"Do you kids live here?"

"Yes, we do."

"Is anybody inside? We need to know before we go in."

"Thank God, not any more."

"You all got out? All of you?"

"Yes. But Ari was in there the longest. My big

sister just got him out."

The firemen rushed into the burning house, while one of them called into his walkie-talkie. "Need med care at scene. Smoke inhalation, slight burns, and mild injuries. Baby and two teens. Over."

"Where are your parents?"

"They're not home."

At the hospital, Aliza and Ari were treated for smoke inhalation, and Aliza's leg was put in a cast. Elan and Aliza were given ointment for their burns. Miri's arm was bandaged with a splint and a sling.

Ari was barely moving. He was full of tubes.

"It's a miracle he survived such a fire," one doctor said.

"He was wrapped in a blanket."

"The blanket was obviously wet, something must have spilled on it."

That was milk, thought Aliza. *Momma gave him a cup before she left. I was supposed to help him drink it. If I had fed him as I was supposed to, I would have also remembered to save him earlier.*

Momma rushed to the hospital as soon as she found out what had happened.

"Aliza, Ari, Miri, how are you? Are you OK?"

"Miri can go home already," a doctor told her. "Aliza will be OK, but we're leaving her overnight for observation. Ari will stay here for a while. He's inhaled a lot of smoke that must be cleared out before we can send him home."

Aliza talked to him quietly at his bedside, and read poems from a nursery rhyme book from the shelf.

"Aliza," Momma said, "I'll stay with Ari for a while so that you can lie down."

"OK, Momma. Do you think he'll be OK?"

"I really hope so. We're all praying for him. In the meantime, be sure to take care of yourself. You'll be able to read to Ari, but you also have to recover."

Momma helped Aliza get into her hospital bed.

"Help me turn over. I want to see Ari."

Aunt Selma invited them to stay with her until their house was fixed up.

The next evening, the family sat down to talk.

"Ari is very, very sick," began Dad with some tension in his voice. "He will be in the hospital for a while. When he comes home, he will need special care."

"Will he be OK?"

"Will he live?"

"Yes, God willing."

"We can help him."

"We will take care of him."

"I can dress and feed him every morning. I'm up first."

"I'll give him a bath at night."

"I can play with him," said Sarah. "He's almost my age."

"Momma and I were thinking," Dad said, "that we could send him to a special dorm for kids like him after a period of rehabilitation. We would see him only once a month, for a weekend. It would make things easier for the rest of you kids."

"A whole month?"

"No! Don't."

"We want him at home."

"Don't send him away."

"I can feed Ari during dinner. Maybe that way he'll forget all the salt I put into his food. I'll also help him with the phyiso – "

"Physiotherapy."

"Yeah."

"They taught me how to take care of kids like Ari. If I can do it with strangers, I can certainly do it with my own brother."

"So teach the rest of us. We all want to help Ari."

"Yes, we do."

"We were so mean to him."

"Baruch has a sister, Becky," Elan chimed in. "They love to take care of her. I can't help but think how much we have to learn from that family."

"Please, Dad. Momma."

"He's our brother."

Are these the same children who resented him so much? Dad and Momma read each other's minds.

"It's lovely to hear you talk this way," said Dad

thoughtfully. "But do you really mean it? We don't want you to keep changing your minds."

"Dad, he's our brother."

Aliza's eyes filled with tears. "Life can be scary. Everything can change in a second. A person can die! Such horrible things could have happened the day of the fire. We were saved by a miracle. We can't be selfish or think only of ourselves."

"Yes, it won't be easy to take care of Ari, but we can do it. We almost lost him."

"He could have died."

"Aliza saved him."

"He's our brother!"

"So what if he has trouble moving. We can help."

"Maybe soon he'll be able to walk and talk a bit."

"This demands a lot of you kids."

"And it means a lot to us," added Momma.

"But we want to."

"We learned a lot from the fire."

"One thing we learned is that matches really are dangerous."

"Yeah, we knew that they were dangerous, but we played with them anyway."

"I'm sorry about the fire."

"Yes, and I'm also sorry that Ari and Aliza and Elan and Miri got hurt because of us."

"It will take a while until we are all healthy again, but the fire did bring us closer together."

"Right. Elan, when you tried to climb up to the window, you said, 'He's my brother and I have to save him.'"

"We were all excited when he was saved."

"'Cuz we love him," said Miri. *There, I said it, and nobody even laughed.*

"And we *want* to help him."

"This way, we'll also be helping you."

"And we'll also get tzumi, because you'll have more time for us."

"Even with Baby Danny."

"So we'll all be happy."

"Too bad we didn't realize this three years ago," Aliza said regretfully.

"Too bad we needed a fire to fix up our family," said Miri. "I'll do my part. I have Show and Tell in a few weeks. I think I'll change my topic. Can I bring in Ari?"

"If he's healthy enough by then."

"And I'll tell all about him, his CP, and how I take care of him. Of course," she lowered her eyes, "I'll also have to kinda change his apple on the family tree."

There was a pause.

"Yeah, and – "

She stopped in mid-sentence, as there was a knock on the door. In walked a newspaper reporter

from the *Jewish Kinder*.

"So where is the star of the show?" he asked.

"He's still in the hospital."

"OK. Before I visit him, I'll get the story from the brave rescue squad."

The children told him about the exciting adventure, while his assistant held the microphone in their faces.

A few minutes later, the reporter turned to Dad and Momma. "Is it okay if you join the kids while we all visit Ari? It's just a short drive from here. We want a picture showing everybody."

When they arrived at the hospital, Momma reminded them, "There are sick people here. Let's try to be very quiet."

"Ari! Hi, Ari."

"Get behind his crib for a picture. Good. I want to see nice smiles. Everybody say 'Gveeeeeeena.' Ooh, there are so many of you. We'll have to have two rows. How many kids are there?"

There was a pause, as all the kids turned towards Dina. She blushed deeply and then glanced up at her family. Then, in the hushed silence, she turned back to the photographer and whispered:

"Seven."

LIKE RUTH AND NAOMI

By Tovah S. Yavin

Tovah S. Yavin

One glorious spring day, I hurried back to my home in Maryland after visiting the National Art Gallery in Washington, D.C. I couldn't wait to tell my husband, two sons, and one daughter about the wonderful thing that I had just seen. (My four dogs and two cats didn't seem interested.) Since then, I have often wondered about the story behind the amazing event I saw that day. I can't be sure, of course, but it might have been just "Like Ruth and Naomi."

Enjoy reading this story and may every one of your days be as life affirming and inspiring for you as that spring day was for me.

LIKE RUTH AND NAOMI

Ahuva paused outside the rabbi's office, picturing in her mind the familiar waiting room on the other side. Secretary's desk to the left, sofa and coffee table behind that, individual chairs along the right wall.

She reread the note in her hand. It said nothing about why Rabbi Kaplan wanted to see her. Mrs. Lieberman, her fourth period teacher, had only smiled and said that Ahuva might as well go now since the class was going to spend the rest of their time working on their projects, anyway.

Ahuva hated being called to the principal's office. In a school as small as the Springville Yeshiva Middle School for Girls, everyone knew what everyone else did. At lunch, people would ask her what Rabbi Kaplan had wanted.

She thought again about the arrangement of the waiting room and decided she would walk in looking to the left, towards the sofa. But if someone was already sitting there, she'd be ready to turn in the other direction.

Ahuva pushed back the thick wave of hair that always hung down in front of her eyes, sucked in her stomach and went in. A seventh grade girl she knew

slightly was slouched across the sofa taking up the whole center section and even had her books spread out on one side of her with a furry, red coat on the other. Ahuva turned, according to plan, then froze. Three of the four chairs on the other side of the room were already taken. The empty one wasn't even on the end.

She could feel the blush coming, and the light-headedness. Were they all staring at her? Ahuva's eyes, or her brain, wouldn't focus. But surely, by now, everyone in the room must have looked up. They must all be watching, wondering who picked out that blouse, why she wasn't taking a seat like a normal person, and that hair – couldn't she do something better with that hair? That's what they were all thinking. Ahuva was sure of it.

A booming voice interrupted her thoughts before she could take another step forward.

"Hi, Ahuva. Come on in."

Ahuva was so surprised that she gasped.

"I'm sorry," Rabbi Kaplan said in a quieter tone. "I didn't mean to startle you. Come on in."

Ahuva settled in the oversized leather chair facing Rabbi Kaplan's desk and wished she could take one of the candies that he always kept for visiting students. Her mouth felt dry and she wasn't sure what would come out if she tried to speak. A candy would help. It would be a little like medicine. But if she took one, the rabbi might think she really ought

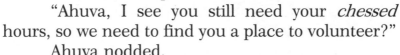

to be watching her diet and then he would disapprove. So Ahuva didn't take the candy. She pushed herself against the back of the chair, crossed her legs and set her right foot waggling, back and forth, to a quick staccato beat.

"Ahuva, I see you still need your *chessed* hours, so we need to find you a place to volunteer?"

Ahuva nodded.

The rabbi shuffled some papers on his desk but didn't actually look at them. "Your grades are excellent and your teachers think you're a wonderful student, as always. But we have to get in these chessed hours before the end of the year. We need to get you started."

Ahuva swallowed and waited.

"Is there something special you'd like to do?"

"Last year, I said *tehillim* for people who were sick." Her voice was barely more than a whisper. If she just had something smooth to suck on.

"Yes. And you did many more than you needed to. I noticed that. I'd like to see you get involved in some other types of activities, though. Mrs. Anderson mentioned that she has some seventh graders who could use help with math. You're very good in math, aren't you?"

Ahuva's foot shifted into a higher gear, back and forth, back and forth.

"I got an A last year," she admitted. "In math,

I mean."

"You get A's every year, Ahuva. In pretty much everything. Would you like to try tutoring?"

She thought about that. Ahuva actually liked doing math, and maybe she could show someone else how to do the problems. But what if they didn't understand her explanations? What if they didn't want to listen?

"I have another idea," the rabbi said. "We have two girls going to the hospital one day a week to visit patients. You just have to say hello and see if you can do anything for them. Then tell them you hope they'll get better soon and that's it."

Rabbi Kaplan smiled at Ahuva and she thought she really would like to do something like that. She could do it, too, if there was someone else with her. But what if the other girl missed a day and she had to go alone. She would never be able to think of anything to say. The patients might yell at her or tell her to go away.

"Well, my mom has to pick me up right after school." That was not exactly a lie. On Tuesdays, her mom really did have to pick her up right after school.

"I see," Rabbi Kaplan nodded. "I think I have just the right idea for you, then." He took a sheet of paper out of his desk and wrote something on it. Then he paused, pulled a note out of his pocket, copied something from that, and shoved the piece of paper across the desk to Ahuva.

She untwisted her legs and scooted forward just enough to reach the piece of paper. The rabbi had written:

> Sarah Goodman
> 157 Brook Lane
> 450-2000

The name seemed familiar, and Ahuva lived at 148 Brook Lane.

"Mrs. Goodman lives down the street from you. Do you know her?"

"I don't think so," Ahuva whispered.

"Her children are in college and her husband's job is quite a distance away. He often gets home late."

Ahuva watched the rabbi, wondering why he was telling her about someone who lived on her street.

"Mrs. Goodman went blind recently. Well, really, she's been losing her sight for years. But this summer... she can barely make out shadows now. With her kids gone, she could use some help. Just with simple jobs around the house and nearby errands."

Ahuva swallowed. "I guess I have to ask Mom."

"Well, actually, I already took the liberty of mentioning a few ideas to your mother and she and

Mrs. Goodman have talked. But it's your choice."

"Okay," Ahuva croaked out her answer. "I can try that."

Ahuva's mother arranged for her to visit Mrs. Goodman on Friday afternoon after school. That left three days to get through two tests and one piano lesson before she had to face this new problem.

She was barely able to study for her history test because her mind kept drifting to Mrs. Goodman. Ahuva had never been around a blind person before. She wasn't sure she would know how to act. Fortunately, her history teacher gave an easy test this time. But her piano lesson went horribly and Mrs. Rodovsky kept shaking her head and saying, "Hmmm."

Finally, it was Friday. After school, Mom told Ahuva not to worry about any of her usual chores and to just go right away to Mrs. Goodman's house.

"You must be Ahuva Silver." Mrs. Goodman opened her front door almost before Ahuva could take her finger off the doorbell. "You don't know how glad I am to see you."

Ahuva could think of nothing to say, which apparently didn't matter, because Mrs. Goodman had hardly paused to take a breath.

"Well, I can't exactly see you, of course. If I could see you, I don't suppose you'd even be here," she said with a laugh that rang of genuine joy. "I have been watching for you. I don't see much, but I watch

all the same. Come in. Come in. You probably want a snack."

"No, I'm fine, Mrs. Goodman. It's okay." Ahuva finally managed to say.

"Good. Good. And I want you to call me Sarah. Just let me get my coat."

Ahuva backed out onto the porch again as Mrs. Goodman... Sarah...seemed to have no trouble finding the coat she wanted from the hall closet. Ahuva wondered where exactly they were going.

Sarah finished buttoning her coat, then pulled a white cane with a red tip from the back of the closet. She set off down the sidewalk and Ahuva scurried to catch up.

"I don't so much need this for myself," Sarah said, as she tapped the cane in front of her. "I can make out buildings and cars. Although I do have trouble with curbs and I fell several times in the beginning. Mostly I carry it so that other people will realize I'm blind and not get offended if I do something annoying." She turned toward Ahuva with a smile. "I also kind of hope other people will see it and be a bit more careful around me."

"Should I...." Ahuva took Sarah's arm. "Should I lead you or something?"

"That would be lovely. But let me show you, dear. Like this." Sarah moved Ahuva's arm so that it was extended in front of her. Then she rested her

own arm on top of Ahuva's with Ahuva slightly in the lead. "Now, you go first. See. It's like those old-fashioned movies where the gentleman leads the lady in to dinner."

"Oh, and I'm the gentleman," Ahuva jokingly complained. "Why can't I be the lady?" Then she realized what she'd just said and how insensitive it must have sounded. "Oh," she gasped. "I'm so sorry. I didn't mean...."

But Sarah just tossed her head back and laughed. "Indeed. Let's trade places sometime." She squeezed Ahuva's arm ever so slightly. "We turn right at the corner, dear."

There was a small grocery store half a block down from the corner. Sarah told Ahuva what she wanted and Ahuva helped her find it. Ahuva didn't really know her way around the store and they ended up going down the same aisles several times. Sarah didn't seem to mind.

Back at the house, Ahuva helped put away the groceries and prepare Shabbat dinner. She turned the oven and the burners to the settings that Sarah told her and handed Sarah spices and other ingredients as she prepared her soup.

It made Ahuva nervous to watch Sarah chop vegetables. She did it entirely by feel without even looking down at her hands. So Ahuva offered to do the cutting and soon everything was ready.

"Thank you so much, Ahuva," Sarah

announced once everything was under
control. "I can't tell you what a help
you've been. How many more chessed
hours do you need?"

"I'm… I'm not sure," Ahuva
stammered. "But I'll keep coming, anyway.
I mean, if you want me to."

"Oh my, yes. That would be just wonderful."

Ahuva quickly said good-bye and hurried out,
because, by then, she was feeling the blush coming
on. She hated blushing. She knew people could tell
and that only made her blush even harder and feel
even more embarrassed.

So she did what she always did. She quickly
turned her back to Sarah, looking down at her feet as
she left. She was halfway to her own house before
she realized that Sarah wouldn't have been able to
tell that she was blushing, anyway.

Ahuva settled into a regular Friday afternoon
routine of helping Sarah get ready for Shabbat. She
learned Sarah's favorite secret recipe for apple-spice
kugel and Sarah soon knew the names of every girl in
Ahuva's class. Ahuva sometimes did last minute
ironing for Sarah and Sarah often listened as Ahuva
reviewed for her weekly science quizzes.

Then there came a Friday afternoon when
Ahuva began to spread out her school books on
Sarah's kitchen table. She was surprised to find a
large, open art book. "What is this?" she asked,

flipping through the pages.

"Oh. That's one of my favorites. Winslow Homer. A wonderful American artist. Did you know that I was an artist?"

Ahuva answered with a shake of her head. Then she caught herself and answered out loud, "No, I didn't."

"Well, maybe I'm flattering myself," Sarah paused from her cooking and smiled. "I only sold a few paintings. Still, it's a bit ironic, isn't it? Like Beethoven going deaf." She turned back to the stove as her smile faded. "But mostly I was an art teacher until a few years ago."

"You were a teacher?"

"I heard on the radio that there was going to be a Winslow Homer exhibit at the art museum downtown. I just love so many of his paintings. So I thought I'd look through the book."

"I could never be a teacher."

"Do you think it's silly that a blind person would want to look at an art book?"

Ahuva shuddered with the chill that suddenly gripped her. "Can you see it at all, Mrs. Goodman?" she whispered.

"Sarah, sweetie. Call me Sarah. I can see a bit of color… and I can make out a shape here or there." She slipped down into the chair next to Ahuva and pointed at the open page. "Tell me what that one is?"

"It's sort of a girl holding a baby chicken. She's

dressed old-fashioned."

"With a bonnet, right? And an apron?"

Ahuva nodded. "Yes," she hurried to add. "Yes."

"I like those. Homer did many American frontier paintings. Find the one with the two little boys going fishing."

Ahuva flipped the pages until she found a picture of two boys, one carrying a long stick and the two of them holding a bucket together. Sarah put her hand out to gently touch the page.

"So, what do you think?" Sarah asked as she stared off in the distance and let her fingers roam around the page. "Do you like it?"

Ahuva leaned in to examine it closely. "I can imagine the worms squiggling around in the bucket."

"Yes! That's just it, isn't it? And you can smell the air, can't you? A fresh, free, grassy smell. Right?"

Ahuva could only smell Sarah's baking *challah*. But she did understand what Sarah meant. The picture drew her in and made her feel almost as if she were there.

"Well," Sarah sighed. "Enough of that." She closed the book and pushed herself up from the table. "I really must get this roast in the oven."

They tucked the book away. Ahuva set the oven temperature and held the door open for Sarah to slip in the pot roast.

"Did you like being a teacher?" Ahuva asked once everything was cooking and the table set.

"Oh my yes. I loved it."

"But... weren't you afraid? Isn't it scary talking to a whole room of people?"

"You know something, Ahuva – I was afraid. Or maybe nervous would be a better word. And I taught for more than 20 years."

"And you never got over it? Being nervous?"

"Not completely. Why, Ahuva? Do you think you'd like to be a teacher?"

"Gosh, no! I could never do that. I hate that. I hate having to get up in front of people."

Sarah set a cup of tea in front of Ahuva and settled down with a cup for herself. "You'd be surprised how many teachers have 'stage fright.' Just like performers. But, you know what, dear?"

Ahuva scooped a spoon of sugar into her tea and waited.

"Once I started talking, I would just forget all about it. If I were showing paintings to my students, I would get so excited about how wonderful they were that all my nervousness just disappeared. Or when I was teaching my classes to draw, I wanted so much for them to be able to make something beautiful and feel good about their work... I didn't even think about being nervous."

"Really?"

Sarah leaned back in her chair. "By the end of

the day, I always felt so wonderful. Tired, but wonderful. I loved the art and I loved sharing it with my students. You could surprise yourself. You might like teaching if you found a subject you really loved."

"Nope. Not me. Never," Ahuva insisted. "I'm going to find a job where I never have to talk to anybody."

Sarah laughed.

But it wasn't funny to Ahuva. To Ahuva, it was all painfully real. It took until the next week for her to get up the nerve to confide in Sarah. They'd finished the shopping and had the soup and the chicken cooking. It was time for their Friday afternoon tea.

"Sarah?" Ahuva began hesitantly.

"Oh! Thank you, dear," Sarah set down her cup before she had a chance to take even a first sip. "How very nice. I do believe that's the first time you've called me Sarah. I'm so glad." She reached across the table and gently patted Ahuva's hand. "You probably don't realize how important you've become to me. I don't just mean with helping out. I mean as a friend."

"I like coming here. I'm glad Rabbi Kaplan thought of it."

"Well, so am I, dear. He's really delightful, isn't he?" Sarah lifted her cup to her lips, but again

set it down without taking a sip. "I interrupted you, didn't I? That's just such a bad habit. I've always interrupted people. But before, I could tell from the look on their faces what I'd done." Sarah stirred her tea even though she hadn't added any sugar. "Now, I just have to remember. What did you want to ask me, dear?"

"It wasn't important...."

"But, of course it was. Please."

"I...um...." Ahuva sighed. "I have to do a report for school. We have to stand up in front of the class and give the report. I hate that. Every year, we have to do that in some class and I just dread it." Ahuva took a breath and went on in a whisper, "Do you... I thought you might have some ideas to help me... you know, since you were a teacher."

"Oh, my," Sarah moved over to sit next Ahuva. "My wonderful young friend. Why are you so shy? Don't you know what a delightful person you are?"

"But, I can't help it," Ahuva insisted. "I hate when people stare at me. I always wonder what they're thinking. Then, I can't talk – I just croak like a frog and my head gets dizzy and I feel so stupid."

Sarah laughed. "You know what, I do have a secret for you. Don't think about what people are thinking. Just think about what you want to say and nothing else. What do you have to report on, anyway?"

"It's not that hard, really. I'm just supposed to

discuss my favorite story from the  *Tanach* and tell what I learned from it. If I could just write it, I wouldn't mind. It's talking in front of everyone that I hate."

"I have an idea, Ahuva. Bring your report next week and you can practice on me. You won't even have to worry about me staring at you," Sarah added with a smile.

Just then, Sarah's grandfather clock rang out and Ahuva knew she had to hurry home.

"I haven't even picked what I'm going to talk about," Ahuva said, gathering her things to leave.

"Well, then, do my favorite story. Wait here." Sarah hurried away.

It was getting late, but Ahuva waited anyway. She checked her watch and wondered if Sarah might need her help finding something. When Sarah reappeared, she had a book in her hand.

"I've read this so many times, I knew what the cover felt like. Bring it next week and I'll help you practice giving your report."

Ahuva took the volume and hurried down the street. Shabbat was coming and she still had chores to do at home. She didn't even notice what book Sarah had given her until she dumped all her school things on her desk. It was the *Book of Ruth*.

On Monday, Mrs. Lieberman wrote each girl's name on the blackboard and the story she had decided to use for her report. Too many girls had picked the story of Esther, so some girls changed and some girls traded until no more than three girls were working on any one story. Girls using the same story were allowed to work together.

Only Ahuva had picked the *Book of Ruth*. She would have to work alone.

Usually, Ahuva preferred working alone. But this time, she wished at least one other person had picked Ruth's story. Then, she could have made posters and someone else could have done the talking.

She explained all of this to Sarah as they strolled down the produce aisles the next Friday afternoon.

"But, couldn't you have just chosen something else, then?" Sarah asked as she sniffed the cantaloupe that Ahuva had just handed her. "This one isn't quite ripe enough, dear. Can you find another one?"

Ahuva picked out another cantaloupe. That one met with Sarah's approval and went into the cart.

"I thought you liked that story," Ahuva protested. "Isn't that why you gave it to me?"

They stopped a short way down the aisle so that Sarah could pick out some tomatoes. "It's not important what I like, though, is it?" Sarah said as she filled the bag that Ahuva held open. "Do you like it?"

"Sure," Ahuva pushed the cart forward, carefully guiding Sarah as they went. "We've studied it before. But I read it again last Shabbat and it just seemed – different – or new – or something. I thought about it all day. Ruth really loved Naomi, didn't she?"

"Oh yes," Sarah nodded. "I always thought so. And she was so trusting."

"Yes. Trusting. She didn't even know what her life would be like with Naomi, but she went anyway."

"Yes, she did," Sarah nodded. "She went, anyway. I'm not sure why I always liked that story so much, but I did. And then when I was losing my sight, I seemed to like it even more."

The shopping was done and Ahuva led Sarah to the front of the store to pay for the groceries. Then, they each took a bag and headed towards Sarah's house.

"Sarah?" Ahuva began. "Did you feel like Ruth? I mean, walking out of your house and not being able to see anything. Was that a little like Ruth going to a life that she didn't know anything about?"

Sarah stopped suddenly. Ahuva took two more steps before she realized she was walking alone and turned back. "Well, I guess so," Sarah said, then started walking again. "I never even thought of it that way. I suppose you're right."

Ahuva guided Sarah up the stairs to her house, then set to work putting away the groceries. Sarah was trying a new recipe this week and kept Ahuva busy searching the pantry for the ingredients she needed.

When all was finished, they discussed Ahuva's report over their afternoon tea.

"You mentioned posters," Sarah said as they talked. "You're supposed to do a poster, too?"

"Well, I can. And if I have a nice poster for everyone to look at, they won't pay so much attention to me." Ahuva sighed. "The problem is, I'm not very artistic."

"Ahh, my dear," Sarah said with a smile. "But I am. Next week, we'll do our shopping on Bryan Avenue. I know of an excellent art supply store, there. We'll make you a beautiful poster."

By the following Friday, Ahuva had sketched out what she wanted to put on her poster. She described it to Sarah, and Sarah suggested colors and how to arrange the information. She also showed Ahuva some old posters that her students had done with beautiful borders and lettering.

When they left Sarah's house, they turned right instead of left. Bryan Avenue was a little farther away than Clarendon, where they usually shopped, and their path took them along busier streets.

People stared. Ahuva noticed that people would glance quickly at them as they approached,

look away for a moment, then look again. She was sure that people were turning back to get a good, long look at their backs, too. She could feel it. She could feel their eyes.

Sarah slowed as they approached the art supply store. "I haven't been here in such a long time," she said. "But I know we're close."

"This is it." Ahuva opened the door and guided Sarah in, glad to be away from all the curious stares.

Sarah took a few steps in, then stopped. She paused in the middle of the small store, breathed deeply, and broke into a wide smile. "Oh, my dear. Doesn't this just smell wonderful? The paints, the chalk. I even think I can smell the paper. My, how I have missed this."

Sarah seemed to know everyone in the store and everyone there seemed to know her. Sales people crowded around Sarah shaking her hand and asking how she'd been. She described Ahuva's project, the type of poster paper, paints, glitter and decorative borders she wanted and people scurried off to find everything that Sarah asked for. In the meantime, Ahuva wandered about the store.

She picked up a flyer announcing the upcoming Winslow Homer exhibit at the museum downtown. It showed small versions of several Homer paintings and one of them was the picture of the two little boys going fishing, the one that Sarah

had asked her to find in the large art book.

"So what do you think, Ahuva?" Sarah called out. "Come and see if the colors seem right to you."

Ahuva joined Sarah at a large counter where one of the sales people had spread out the materials collected for her poster. A young man started to explain to her how the color for the border would complement the color of paint that Sarah had picked for the lettering. He also spread out an arrangement of paintbrushes pointing out which ones to use for lettering and which for filling in background colors.

Ahuva listened a little. Mostly, she watched Sarah moving about the store, tapping her cane. She found her way to a back corner to a large display of posters in plastic coverings.

Sarah flipped through them, asking an older man who had joined her what each one was.

She lingered over some of the posters. That corner of the store received no sunlight and Sarah didn't even try to see them. She didn't move in close to squint as she sometimes did at home to try and see whatever she could of things.

Instead, Sarah gazed off in the opposite direction while flipping through the posters. "What is this one?" she would ask. Then she would say, "Oh, yes. Of course. Of course," when the answer was given.

"How does that seem to you? Do you like it?" the young man asked Ahuva. Maybe, it was the

second time he had asked her, or the
third. Ahuva wasn't sure. She had only
been listening a little.

"Fine. It seems fine. I don't
really... I'm not... if Sarah picked it, I'm
sure it will be fine."

The young man nodded and began packaging
all the things. They made the purchase and went
next door for Sarah's groceries. Back at Sarah's
house, they cooked dinner and planned the poster at
the same time. Sarah showed Ahuva how to trace a
map showing Ruth's path from Moav to Naomi's
home in Bethlehem. She told her what colors to use
for the map and where to put the lettering.

Ahuva wanted to tell the class about the
character traits Ruth's actions could teach. She
wanted to talk about love and trust and how loving
someone could help you find the courage to do things
you otherwise might never be able to do. Sarah
helped her plan what to write and gave her stencils to
help with the lettering. They added some glitter and
bordering. Ahuva could see the poster was going to
turn out beautiful even before it was finished.

They worked so long on the poster that they
never even took time for their usual Friday afternoon
tea. When Ahuva walked home, she took the almost-
finished poster and a bag with the brushes and paints
so she could do the lettering later. But she got home
so late, that there was barely enough time to do her

chores and get ready for Shabbat. The poster would have to wait until Saturday night.

She propped it up in her room where she could look at it. Even without the lettering, Ahuva could tell this poster was going to be very special. All evening, she kept sneaking back upstairs to her room to pull back her curtains and admire the poster as it glittered in the silver moonlight

All eyes would be on this poster when she gave her report. Sarah had helped her add so many interesting touches – small pictures cut and pasted in the corners, decorative designs, interesting colors – that no one would have time to look at her.

Ahuva was excited now about giving her report. She could hardly wait for it to be her turn. She was thinking so much about the finishing touches, and the things she wanted to say about the story of Ruth that she almost forgot to check her pockets before setting out the next morning with her family to walk to synagogue.

It was Shabbat and Jewish law forbade her from carrying anything. She had taken one step onto the porch before she remembered to feel in her pockets for a forgotten tissue or stray paper clip. What she felt was a folded up square of paper.

Ahuva stepped back in the house and dropped the paper on the table in their front hall. Then, she remembered what it was. It was the flyer she had picked up at the art store – the one announcing the

Winslow Homer exhibition.

Ahuva thought about that flyer and that art exhibit all the rest of the day. That afternoon, she checked the dates on the calendar. The show was going on next week during days when Ahuva's school was taking a break for teachers' meetings.

She asked her mother where the art museum was. It was all the way downtown, but there was a bus that stopped right near their house that went to the subway, which, in turn, went almost to the art museum. Mom didn't ask why Ahuva wanted to know.

Ahuva wasn't even sure herself why she wanted to know. But she couldn't get the art museum, the Winslow Homer exhibit, or Sarah out of her mind.

When Ahuva walked into Mrs. Lieberman's class Monday morning, she saw a schedule had been tacked to the bulletin board showing when each girl was to give her talk. Ahuva's name was down for Wednesday. That was the last day of school for the week. On Thursday and Friday, school would be closed for the teachers' meetings.

By Tuesday night, most of the reports had been given and Ahuva thought they'd all been wonderful. Some people had made puppets of the characters that they were talking about. Some people had drawn diagrams. Everyone had talked in a clear voice and said interesting things. That was all that Ahuva could think about Tuesday night.

How was her report going to come out? Would the class laugh at her poster? Would they yawn while she talked?

The next day, Mrs. Lieberman smiled as Ahuva walked toward the front of the room. She helped Ahuva prop her poster up against the blackboard. Before she backed away to let Ahuva begin her report, she had peered closely at the map, raised her eyebrows and nodded. It seemed to Ahuva that she liked the poster.

"Um...I'm going to talk about the story of Ruth," Ahuva began. She stared down at her shoes. "And um... she was married to Naomi's son... and um...."

"Excuse me, Ahuva," Mrs. Lieberman interrupted. "Before you begin, can you tell us why you decided to do this particular story? Why Ruth?"

"Oh, because Ruth was such a special person," Ahuva looked up, focusing on Mrs. Lieberman. "I know we've all read the story before. And I don't think I ever thought so much about it before. But then, when I reread the story, all I could think about was how brave Ruth was. Don't you think she was afraid when she followed Naomi to a strange place and a strange new life? Wouldn't that be scary?"

Mrs. Lieberman smiled and nodded.

"But she did it anyway because she just loved Naomi so much. And she trusted her. When you love someone, you trust them, don't you? And Naomi, too. She was wonderful, too. She lived up to that trust, I think. She took care of Ruth and made sure she could have a good life."

Ahuva looked around, now. The class seemed to be listening closely. Some girls had their notebooks open and their pens in their hands. Ahuva began explaining the whole story of Ruth. She pointed to her map and noticed girls nodding, writing, watching intently.

When she finished, Mrs. Lieberman allowed the girls to come up a few at a time for a close look at Ahuva's poster. While they were doing that, she filled out the evaluation form for Ahuva's report and handed it to her. Mrs. Lieberman gave her an A. At the bottom of the form she had written, "Very well thought out report. Excellent visual aid."

Ahuva had thought that she would spend her Thursday off from school sleeping late. But, when she came home from school on Wednesday, she discussed a different plan with her mother.

The whole idea was scary. Mom took out a map and wrote out careful instructions. She made some calls so Ahuva would know exactly which bus and subway to take and how much money to have with her. Then, before she could have second

thoughts, Ahuva placed the call.

"Sarah?"

There was a pause at the other end and then Sarah's voice. "Ahuva! You surprised me. I'm not used to hearing from you except on Fridays. How did your report go?"

"It was fine. Actually, I think my teacher really liked it. I got an A." Ahuva hadn't meant to brag about the report, but she couldn't help herself.

"Oh, my dear, that's wonderful. I'm so proud of you."

"Sarah, I actually called about something else." Ahuva's hand was shaking, but Sarah couldn't know that, could she? She took a deep breath and went on. "Do you remember that Winslow Homer exhibit? At the museum? You told me about it, remember?"

"But of course, dear. It's this week, I believe."

"Would you like to go, Sarah? I mean, I could take you." Ahuva slipped down into the chair next to the phone. "That is, I'd like to take you." She waited and Sarah said nothing.

Suddenly, Ahuva began to think about how crazy her idea was. Who would take a blind person to an art museum? Would Sarah think Ahuva was making fun of her or being mean to her?

Until just now, it had seemed like such a wonderful idea. She had thought about how Sarah had touched the art book even though she couldn't

see the pictures. She remembered how Sarah had stood next to the posters in the art store wanting to know what each one was. Somehow, Ahuva had thought that Sarah would like to be there – at the art museum – even if she couldn't see the paintings. Had she been totally wrong? If Sarah would just say something....

There was only silence on the other end of the line.

"Oh – my, dear," Sarah finally breathed into the phone. "Oh, my dear. Oh, my. I never thought... the idea just never.... Oh, my dear."

Ahuva waited. There were a hundred things she wanted to say. She wanted to say she certainly had never meant to embarrass Sarah. She wanted to say it had just seemed to her Sarah might like to be there and after all, Sarah had done so much for her, had become such a good friend. But she didn't say any of that. She just waited.

"Well, yes. Well, yes, of course. Oh, I would love that. My goodness, how on earth will we manage it? I don't even know how to...."

"But I know, Sarah. My mother helped me figure it all out. We'll take the bus and then...."

Ahuva and Sarah talked for an hour to get all the arrangements straight. Ahuva took some of that time to tell Sarah more about her report, what the teacher had said, and how everyone in the class had

listened and taken notes. She mentioned she wasn't even nervous. At least, not very nervous.

They set out together early the next morning. The walk to the bus station was not much different from their usual walk to the market on Fridays. It was a fresh, snappy Thursday morning, a little after rush hour. Ahuva held out one arm to guide Sarah and kept her other hand in her pocket where she could feel the sheet of instructions that her mom had written out for her.

They passed very few people as they walked. Ahuva didn't bother to notice if anyone stared at them or twisted to look back as they walked by. No one was waiting at the bus stop. Sarah and Ahuva settled on the smoothy worn wooden bench to wait for the bus.

When it came, Ahuva led Sarah up the steps and into a front seat, then went back to pay the driver. He took her money and acted as if kids often rode his bus with blind friends.

The subway station was very different. The bus pulled up in a circular drive and dispatched them right in front of the station. Even at 10:00 in the morning, it was a busy place. A line of people waited for Ahuva and Sarah to get off so they could file onto the bus.

As Ahuva led Sarah into the station, she noticed heads turning. A child tugged at her mother's arm and pointed at them. She had to let

Sarah stand by herself for a moment while she bought their tickets from a machine against a far wall.

Ahuva glanced toward Sarah as she waited her turn. People were openly watching her. As if it didn't matter. As if no one could tell Sarah later that she was being stared at. As if Sarah wouldn't care and wouldn't blush or feel embarrassed by all of those eyes. Of course, Sarah didn't blush and Ahuva knew she would never tell Sarah anything about all that curiosity.

When they finally arrived downtown, the streets were too busy for anyone to notice Sarah or for Ahuva to pay attention to what anyone else was noticing. She followed her mother's instructions and easily found the art museum. Sarah had said almost nothing the whole way. She had worn dark glasses, something she rarely did, and had sat silently through the entire trip twisting a handkerchief in her hands.

Ahuva didn't need to ask where the Winslow Homer exhibit was. She just followed the crowd. Sarah tightened her grip on Ahuva's arm as they entered a crowded room and began to move slowly from painting to painting.

"Should I describe the pictures?" Ahuva whispered.

"Oh, yes. Please," Sarah answered just as quietly.

"Okay – well," Ahuva paused and glanced around her. "This one shows soldiers...."

She tried to explain the pictures as best she could. She tried to talk quietly so only Sarah would hear. People began to move aside for them. They smiled, and opened up pathways, allowing Ahuva to lead Sarah as close to the paintings as visitors were allowed to go.

Ahuva noticed, occasionally, that people were pausing to listen, too. Sarah leaned in towards Ahuva's voice and interrupted her with questions.

"But what color is the sky? What are the people doing? Am I close to it?"

Sarah asked that question often, "Am I close to it? Where? Is it to my right? Is it next to me?"

Sarah seemed to want to be near the pictures. She wanted to know where they were and how close the paintings were to her.

"Oh, I just love being here," Sarah said as they waited their turn to see more of the paintings in another room. "Doesn't it feel special coming so close to this wonderful art?"

Ahuva nodded. Of course, she knew very well by now that you shouldn't nod around a blind person. How could they tell? But she did it, anyway, and Sarah always seemed to know. And today, especially, Ahuva thought that Sarah could sense what she, herself, was feeling. It felt to her like they were together, today. Not just next to each other. But

together. Two friends enjoying something very special, together.

"Oh, I like these!" Ahuva announced as she drew Sarah towards a wall lined with pictures of children and a schoolhouse. "There's a teacher and all the kids are sitting on benches around the walls."

"Of course. Of course. Those are very famous. Is there one with little boys playing outside?"

"Umm. Yes, over there," Ahuva brought Sarah close to that picture. "The children are holding hands and...."

"That's called 'Snap the Whip'. Right?"

"Yes, it says..."

"That one is very well known. It's a game that kids used to play. And isn't the sky lovely in that one? And there are flowers, aren't there?"

Ahuva just waited because Sarah seemed to be able to see the painting in her memory even better than Ahuva could see it right before her eyes.

"Oh, but don't they have the one with the teacher looking out a window while the children are playing outside?"

Ahuva searched the room until she spotted the one Sarah was talking about.

"Are we there?" Sarah asked. "Is this it?"

Ahuva didn't bother to answer with anything other than the softest touch to Sarah's shoulder.

"I think I always loved this one more than any

131

of his other works, more than almost any other painting. Doesn't it look like the teacher wishes she could go outside and play with the kids? That's what I always thought about this one. We teachers like a little fresh air, too, sometimes." Sarah laughed. She lingered for the longest time. Other people politely moved around them. No one shoved. Finally, Sarah patted Ahuva's arm and turned away. "That was always my favorite. Thank you so much, dear. This has been such fun."

Ahuva led the way outside, to the subway, the bus, and finally, Sarah's front door. Then she walked, or floated, home. It felt more like floating. She couldn't remember when she had felt happier.

Mom wanted to know everything as soon as Ahuva stepped in the front door. She tried to explain how Sarah's face had looked as they wandered among all those gorgeous paintings. Sarah had looked more than happy. Maybe, at times, she had even looked a little sad. But Ahuva understood that it was a good kind of sad. And she knew that Sarah had had a wonderful experience because of her.

Mom never said "But Ahuva. How could you have done all that? It's so unlike you." Ahuva waited and Mom never even said it. She just smiled and fixed all of Ahuva's favorite foods for dinner.

By the next morning, Ahuva had made another decision. She thought more about it that afternoon while she and Sarah went through their

usual routine, and she thought about it all day Shabbat and Sunday. She knew it would be hard. Maybe one of the hardest things she had ever done. But the decision was made and Ahuva was determined to carry out her plan at the first possible chance on Monday.

But Monday was busy. The first day back after a long weekend was always busy and it seemed as if Ahuva would never get her chance. Class after class went by and she worried that maybe she would lose her nerve.

Finally, lunchtime came. Ahuva made her way to the cafeteria and looked around. Spotting Debra was easy. Debra always sat in a back corner with an open book in front of her. Ahuva knew that because she always sat in a corner with an open book, too. Ahuva knew all the tricks for when you wanted to be alone, or when you thought that nobody really wanted to sit with you, anyway, and it was better to look like you preferred to be alone.

"Hi, Debra. Is that good?" Ahuva pointed at the open book. "I've been thinking of reading it, too."

"Yeah," Debra answered slowly. "It's pretty good. I guess."

"Do you mind if I sit down?" Debra nodded and Ahuva took the seat across from her. "Do you have all your chessed hours done, yet?"

Debra just shook her head.

"Um. I don't either. I was thinking about tutoring some younger girls. I think someone said there were seventh graders that could use tutoring. Like in math or English. But the thing is...." Ahuva cleared her throat. "The thing is, I'm kind of scared to do it alone."

"Really," Debra leaned back and closed her book. "Because I might like to do that. I'm good in English. But I didn't want to go by myself, either."

"So I was thinking...."

"Maybe, we could do it together?" Debra interrupted and Ahuva breathed a sigh of relief.

"Yeah. We could do it together. Do you want to go tell Rabbi Kaplan, now? In case," Ahuva smiled. "In case, one of us changes our minds."

By the time Friday rolled around again, Ahuva and Debra had done more than work together tutoring younger students. They had become friends. Ahuva could not remember ever having reached out to anyone like that before. She had friends, but they had always been the ones to start the friendship. This time, Ahuva had started the friendship and she was proud of herself for doing it.

She could hardly wait to tell Sarah.

"I have the best news!" Ahuva announced as soon as she stepped in the front door of Sarah's house that Friday afternoon.

"Oh, my goodness. What could it be?" Sarah settled on the sofa and waited with a pleased smile."

"I made a friend this week." Ahuva was so excited she didn't notice the empty bookcase next to the rocking chair where she sat facing Sarah. "I know that doesn't sound like such a big deal. But it is for me. She's really nice. And we like a lot of the same things and we're doing tutoring together. You were right. Teaching is fun."

Ahuva paused to take a breath, then went on talking without noticing the boxes stacked next to the dining room table.

"I could never have done it without you. I've done things these last few weeks that I never thought I could. I gave that report at school. And we went to the art museum which I thought would be scary but it was fun. And then I met Debra. We even call each other at night to talk about homework."

"I'm so glad, honey. You just didn't realize what a good friend you could be."

"What are those boxes, Sarah?" Ahuva stood and looked around the room. "Where are all your books?"

"Well, I have news, too." Sarah spoke much more quietly than Ahuva had. "We've decided to move."

"Move?"

"There's a house near my sister and it's closer to my husband's work. It's smaller than this house, but the kids are gone most of the time now, anyway."

"You're moving?"

"Oh, sweetie," Sarah held out her arms and Ahuva came to sit next to her on the sofa. "Don't be sad. You see, my news is because of our friendship, too. Just like your news."

"I don't understand." Ahuva's voice trembled.

"After you took me to the museum – oh, my dear – you just don't know what that meant to me. I realized there's so much of life that I am missing. I thought, when I really couldn't see any more, that I could manage with just a little help. But you showed me I was cheating myself. I really need more help and my sister has been begging me to move closer."

"Sarah, I don't want you to leave."

"Oh, Ahuva. My sweet Ahuva." Sarah wrapped her arm around Ahuva's shoulder and drew her close. "We're a little like Ruth and Naomi, aren't we? I'll never forget you." A tear slipped from Ahuva's face, falling lightly on Sarah's arm. "And I'm so glad that I was able to make a difference in your life, too."

Ahuva leaned in against the warmth of Sarah's body. Sarah squeezed Ahuva lightly, then gently eased herself free and stood. She motioned for Ahuva to stand, too.

"But I'm not leaving today," she said. "And we still have Shabbat to make."

So, that's what Sarah and Ahuva did. They prepared for Shabbat, just as they had every Friday

afternoon for all those weeks. They
shopped. They baked. They cooked.
And they helped each other.

Just like Ruth and Naomi.

NOAH'S CHOICE

By Michele Order Litant

Michele Order Litant

Michele Order Litant is an editor of children's books and teachers' guides at Sundance Publishing. Previously, she worked in an elementary school library. She is the founder and coordinator of a children's writers' critique group and has been writing since the age of ten. She lives in Massachusetts with her husband and two sons.

"There are many kinds of love stories in life. Some children are lucky to have a special relationship with a grandparent. NOAH'S CHOICE is loosely based on my own experience with my younger son and his Bar Mitzvah."

140

NOAH'S CHOICE

Noah stared at his mother in shock. He couldn't believe what she had just told him. It couldn't possibly be true. But Mom was crying.

"He didn't suffer, Noah. Bubbie says that by the time the ambulance came, Zaydie was already gone. It was a heart attack."

Zaydie was dead? How could that be? What would Noah do now?

"But what about my Bar Mitzvah?" Noah asked. "Who's going to help me now?"

Mom stared at Noah for a minute before she replied. "Noah, I know you're upset and you're not thinking clearly. But your Bar Mitzvah is not the most important thing right now. I'm upset, too. Zaydie was my father. This is so unexpected, we're all in shock. We can't worry about your Bar Mitzvah right now."

"Maybe you can't, but I can!" Noah yelled. "I can't study without Zaydie. He taught me to read Hebrew. He was going to help me practice my Torah portion. Who's going to help me now? I can't have a Bar Mitzvah without Zaydie and you don't even care!"

Noah ran upstairs to his bedroom, slammed the door, and flung himself onto his bed. He tried to

hold back his tears. At thirteen, he was too old to cry, wasn't he? But he couldn't help it. He felt terrible. He'd never felt so bad in his whole life. He suddenly understood what a broken heart was, because his hurt so much it felt like it could break. He couldn't believe, didn't want to believe, that Zaydie was dead. Zaydie wasn't just his grandfather, he was his best friend.

He hadn't meant to sound selfish, but one of the reasons he'd decided to have a Bar Mitzvah was because Zaydie was going to help him prepare for it. Noah had quit Hebrew school at the end of third grade after he learned about the bargain his parents had made. When Noah was in kindergarten, his mother wanted to send him to Hebrew school. But his father said no—he'd hated being forced to go himself and refused to force his son to go. But when Noah came home from kindergarten one day crying because all of his friends celebrated Christmas and he didn't, Dad realized that Noah needed to spend time with other Jewish children. He made a deal with Mom that she could send Noah to Hebrew school as long as he wanted to go. If Noah hated it and didn't want to go, he didn't have to. Mom didn't think that Noah should have a choice about this, but she reluctantly agreed.

About halfway through the third grade, Noah complained to his father about how much he hated going to Hebrew school. He was surprised when Dad

told him he didn't have to go if he really didn't want to.

"But isn't it like regular school? You just have to go?" asked Noah.

"No," answered Dad. "Hebrew school is something you should choose to do to learn about Judaism. I don't see the point in forcing you to go. You won't learn anything. Your mother disagrees with me. She thinks it's important for you to go, to learn about your Jewish heritage and to be with other Jewish kids."

"But I learn about Jewish things from you and Mom," Noah said. "And I don't care about the kids at Hebrew school. None of them are my friends. None of them go to my regular school. I hate Hebrew school. It's boring."

"Well, Noah, I understand how you feel. I felt the same way when I was your age. That's why your mother and I made a deal. We agreed to send you to Hebrew school but if you hated it, you wouldn't have to go."

"Really? Well, I do hate it," said Noah. "I don't want to go anymore."

"The school year's almost over," said Dad. "Why don't you finish the year and if you still feel this way in the fall, you don't have to start fourth grade. And whether you have a Bar Mitzvah or not will be your choice too."

In the fall, Noah chose not to continue Hebrew

school claiming he didn't want to have a Bar Mitzvah.

But a few months before his thirteenth birthday, his feelings began to change. At first it was because the two other Jewish kids in his sixth grade class were having Bar Mitzvahs. Noah's friends were all asking him if he was having one. He felt uncomfortable saying no, as if his friends would think he was weird or bad. So he said maybe, and the more he said maybe, the more he began to think he really would have a Bar Mitzvah.

Noah began cautiously asking Zaydie questions like, "Do you have to be able to read Hebrew to have a Bar Mitzvah?"

"Of course," said Zaydie. "Becoming Bar Mitzvah means reading from the Torah. And the Torah is written in Hebrew. Why do you ask?"

"Oh, nothing," said Noah. "Aaron and Dan are starting Bar Mitzvah lessons and I just wondered if they had to do everything in Hebrew."

"Well, the prayers and the Torah portion will all be in Hebrew. There might be a few readings in English. But mostly it will be Hebrew. But that shouldn't be a problem for Dan and Aaron since they go to Hebrew school, right?"

"Yeah, right," Noah said, then quickly changed the subject.

The next time Noah saw Zaydie, he asked, "How hard is it to learn to read Hebrew?"

"It's not easy," said Zaydie, "but it's not

impossible. You have to learn a whole new alphabet. But it's just a matter of decoding symbols. When you learned to read English, you had to learn to decode the symbols, the letters of the alphabet. It might be a little harder to learn Hebrew now because you're used to English. But with practice, you certainly could do it."

"I didn't say I wanted to," said Noah quickly. "I was just wondering. You know, because Aaron and Dan are practicing for their Bar Mitzvahs."

"Oh, right," said Zaydie, smiling to himself. "Aaron and Dan."

Zaydie knew Noah well enough to guess that something was on his mind. And Noah knew Zaydie well enough to guess Zaydie suspected there was another reason for the questions he'd been asking lately.

Noah was Zaydie's first grandchild and they had always had a special bond. From the time Noah was born, they'd spent a lot of time together. They always found something special to do, just the two of them. When Noah was really little, they went to the park or the library and got ice cream afterward. After Noah learned to read, they spent a lot of time at bookstores. Both Noah and Zaydie loved science fiction. Noah picked out contemporary sci-fi books for kids and after he read them, he gave them to Zaydie to read. As Noah got older, Zaydie introduced

him to some of the authors he loved, such as Isaac Asimov and Ray Bradbury. They spent hours discussing the books they read.

They'd been playing miniature golf together for a couple of years when Zaydie announced the N & Z Miniature Golf Tournament.

"You know, Noah, now that you're ten, I think you're old enough to enter a tournament," Zaydie said. It was the first day of summer vacation and they were on their way to their favorite miniature golf course.

"What do you mean, Zaydie?" Noah asked. "What tournament?"

"The one I just thought of. The N & Z World Class Miniature Golf Tournament. I was just remembering how last summer you actually beat me a couple of times." Even when Noah was little, Zaydie had never let him win at anything – board games, shooting baskets, mini golf. Zaydie always played his best and Noah had to play his best to beat him. And, whenever he did beat Zaydie, Noah knew it was because he had played better than Zaydie, not because Zaydie had let him win. It meant more to Noah to win based on his own skill.

"If I let you win, you won't learn to try your best," Zaydie had explained when Noah was little. "And if you don't try your best in whatever you do, you won't get far in this world. No one is ever going to just let you win, whether it's a test in school or a job

interview when you get older. You always have
to earn what you win. That's why I'll never let
you win. If you beat me at a game, it'll be
because you earned it."

Noah never minded when he lost to
Zaydie because Zaydie never made a big deal
out of winning. The point was that they were
doing something together and being with Zaydie was
always fun.

Zaydie never treated Noah like he was a baby
or a little boy. From the time Noah could talk, Zaydie
spoke to him like an adult. They had serious
conversations about everything from the best way to
dig in the sand, to whether or not the sci-fi stories
they read could ever become reality. Zaydie listened
to Noah and considered his opinions seriously. He
never disregarded anything Noah said just because
he was a kid.

When Zaydie suggested the miniature golf
tournament, Noah was excited. He knew Zaydie
wouldn't have told him about it unless he thought
Noah had a chance of winning.

"How will it work, Zaydie?" Noah asked.

"Well," said Zaydie, "we'll just play this
summer like we always do. But each time we play,
we'll write the winner's name on the front of the
scorecard and we'll save all the scorecards. At the
end of the summer, we'll count up how many games
each of us won, and the person who won the

most will be the N & Z World Class Miniature Golf Tournament champion. What do you think?"

"Cool," said Noah, smiling at Zaydie. Zaydie always thought of such fun things to do. He never thought Noah was too young to do anything. Take reading, for example. When Noah was eleven, he had mentioned to Zaydie during one of their visits to the library that he couldn't find anything to read in the children's room anymore. Zaydie had taken him to the adult section and helped him find some books.

When they got home, Noah's mom said, "Do you think he's old enough to be reading adult books, Dad?"

"Listen," said Zaydie. "When you were his age, the same thing happened. You'd read all of the books in the children's room so I took you to the adult section. And your mother asked me the same thing you're asking me. So, I'll tell you the same thing I told her. Noah can read whatever he wants. If it's too adult and he doesn't understand it, he won't be interested, and he won't read it."

Zaydie had always been Noah's ally, had always supported Noah in everything he did. Except when Noah quit Hebrew school. That was the only time Noah ever felt that Zaydie was disappointed in him. It was the only time they ever disagreed.

"What do you mean you're quitting Hebrew school? School isn't a choice," said Zaydie.

Noah explained, "My dad says I don't have to

go if I don't want to. He hated being forced to
go when he was a kid so he doesn't want to
force me. I hate it, Zaydie. It's so boring
and I'm tired after school. I don't get home
from Hebrew school until 6:00 P.M. and then
I still have homework to do from regular
school."

"But it's only one day a week, Noah. Your
mother went to Hebrew school five days a week.
Surely you can deal with it once a week."

"I don't want to go anymore, and my dad says
I don't have to."

"I don't understand why your parents are
letting you decide. Since when is school a choice?"

"Mom thinks I should go. But Dad says it's up
to me. He says you don't have to go to Hebrew school
or synagogue to be a Jew."

"Maybe not," said Zaydie. "But an important
part of Judaism is being part of a Jewish community.
It's important for you to be with other Jewish kids.
It's important for you to learn about your religion and
culture."

"I learn about Jewish stuff from Mom and Dad,
and from you and Bubbie. I like all the things we do
for the holidays. I don't learn anything at Hebrew
school. And I don't care about being with those kids.
None of them are my friends. They don't go to my
regular school."

"What about learning to read Hebrew? How

149

will you become Bar Mitzvah if you can't read Hebrew?"

"I don't want to have a Bar Mitzvah," said Noah.

Zaydie just stared at Noah for a minute. Then he turned and looked out the window.

Noah was surprised and confused. Was Zaydie angry? There was a look on his face Noah had never seen there before. It took him a minute to realize it was sadness. Zaydie was sad and it was because of Noah. Noah couldn't bear to think that Zaydie was disappointed in him. Finally, Zaydie turned back and reached an arm out to Noah. With relief, Noah snuggled up to him.

"When I was a boy," Zaydie said, "I didn't have a choice. My parents sent me to Hebrew school, and when I was twelve, I started studying with the rabbi for my Bar Mitzvah. When my father, your great-grandfather, was a boy in Russia, he had to study secretly.

"You didn't advertise the fact you were Jewish back then. Jews were mistreated, persecuted. Eventually Jews were rounded up and made to live in ghettos, confined areas. So my father studied in secret and he became Bar Mitzvah in secret. Not in a synagogue. The synagogue had been destroyed by Russian soldiers. My father read from the Torah in the cellar of a store owned by a sympathetic Christian who gave the Jews of the village a place to worship.

"My parents escaped from Russia and came to America with my brother and two sisters. Four more of us children were born here. My parents felt so lucky, so privileged to be able to send their sons to Hebrew school in freedom. They felt privileged to be able to walk openly into *shul*, synagogue, to witness their sons become Bar Mitzvah.

"I never questioned going to Hebrew school or having a Bar Mitzvah. I didn't like going to Hebrew school, but my parents sent me, and I went. You, Noah, are questioning why you should go. Studying Torah is an important part of Judaism. However, Jews are not expected to blindly accept the teachings of the Torah. A good Jew questions and uses his intelligence to interpret the laws of the Torah. So your questioning is a good thing. However, I question whether at nine years old you have enough information to make such a big decision. So I have a favor to ask you, Noah."

"What, Zaydie?"

"Will you keep open the possibility of a Bar Mitzvah? Keep an open mind and think about what being Jewish means to you. Maybe when you're thirteen you still won't feel the need to have a Bar Mitzvah. But maybe by then you will want to. Whatever you decide, I love you and am proud of you. You're a good person and that's what makes a good Jew. Do you know what Bar Mitzvah means, Noah?"

"No, Zaydie. What does it mean?"

"It means *one who has the obligation of fulfilling a mitzvah*. Mitzvah refers to the commandments God gave to Moses. It also means a good deed, doing things to help others."

"Like when we bring food and clothes to the food pantry for poor people," said Noah.

"That's right," said Zaydie. "That's a mitzvah."

"Okay. I'll think about it," said Noah. "But I'm not going to Hebrew school anymore. So I don't know how I'll have a Bar Mitzvah if I can't read Hebrew."

"Noah, when the time comes, if you decide you want to become Bar Mitzvah, it will be my great honor and joy to teach you to read Hebrew. Deal?"

"Deal," said Noah, hugging Zaydie. "I love you, Zaydie. You're the best."

Noah didn't think about a Bar Mitzvah after that until he was in sixth grade. When his classmates, Aaron and Dan, told everyone the date of their Bar Mitzvahs, naturally, the kids asked Noah, the only other Jewish kid in the class, when his Bar Mitzvah would be.

"Um, I don't know yet," said Noah, surprising himself. He couldn't seem to say that he wasn't having one.

"How come you don't know, but Aaron and Dan know?" asked Matt.

"They go to a different synagogue," said Noah.

"Well, are you having a Bar Mitzvah?" asked Shane.

"Maybe.   I don't know," mumbled Noah.

"Don't you have to have one if you're Jewish?" asked Matt.

"Well, you usually do," said Noah. "But my parents said it's up to me." He was starting to feel uncomfortable. It was hard enough being Jewish and always having to explain why he didn't celebrate Christmas or Easter. But it was a lot harder to explain why he wasn't celebrating what his friends knew was an important Jewish tradition.

Noah began to question why he didn't want to have a Bar Mitzvah. At first, it had been because he didn't want to go to Hebrew school and he just figured that if he didn't go to Hebrew school, he wouldn't have a Bar Mitzvah.   But now he remembered that conversation with Zaydie and the deal they'd made.

"...It will be my great honor and joy to teach you to read Hebrew. Deal?" Zaydie had said.

Zaydie hadn't mentioned it since that time, but Noah knew the deal was still good.   He appreciated the fact that over the past few years Zaydie hadn't brought up the subject of a Bar Mitzvah, hadn't nudged him or tried to talk him into

it. That was one of the things Noah loved about Zaydie. Zaydie never tried to tell Noah what to do. Noah knew Zaydie wanted him to have a Bar Mitzvah. But he hadn't tried to talk Noah into it.

But now his friends were asking him about having a Bar Mitzvah, he thought more and more about that conversation with Zaydie. It hadn't meant much to him at the time, but now he thought about his great-grandfather, Nathan, who had his Bar Mitzvah in secret. What did that mean? Why would anyone have to study Hebrew and have a Bar Mitzvah in secret? How could anyone tell you you couldn't practice your own religion? What would have happened to Nathan if he'd been caught?

Noah remembered what Zaydie had said about how Nathan felt privileged to walk openly into a synagogue and see his sons become Bar Mitzvah in freedom. What must that have felt like, after hiding his religion for so many years?

Noah couldn't imagine not being able to admit he was Jewish. Sure, there were times it was kind of embarrassing. It was hard to be different when all of his friends were Christians. It was hard to have to explain every year why he didn't celebrate their holidays. And they had no idea what the Jewish holidays were all about.

That's why, since he was in kindergarten, his mom would come in to his classroom every year to read a holiday story and share a traditional treat with

his classmates. On Hanukkah, she'd bring in a menorah and dreidels. The kids loved learning how to play dreidel. On Purim, Mom would bring in *hamentashen* Noah had helped bake. The kids looked forward to them so much that every September, the kids lucky enough to be in the same class as Noah would ask him, "Are you going to bring those special cakes in this year?"

Noah liked how much his classmates appreciated and enjoyed the parts of his culture he shared with them. He always felt left out when the Christian holidays took place. He felt good when he talked about a Jewish holiday and the kids were interested. They were happy to learn about and share his traditions. And they all knew that a Bar Mitzvah is a Jewish tradition. He could tell that they seemed puzzled when he said he might not have one. Would they think he wasn't a good Jew?

Noah began to wonder himself. If he didn't have a Bar Mitzvah, would he not be a good Jew? Being Jewish was important to Noah. He didn't feel particularly religious. He wasn't sure he believed in God.

But the Jewish traditions were important to him, the holidays and all of the customs. His mother lit the Shabbat candles every Friday night, and Noah said the blessing over the challah. Each holiday had its rituals and special foods. These traditions were

important to Noah. They were part of who his family was, who he was.

He knew that a Bar Mitzvah is a Jewish tradition. If Jewish traditions were important to him, would he feel right, as a Jew, not having a Bar Mitzvah? He'd be the only boy in his family not to have one. And that would include his great-grandfather Nathan who had to have his secretly, had to hide the fact that he was a Jew. Noah was named in honor of Nathan. He had the same Hebrew name as Nathan — Nachman Dovid. If Noah had a Bar Mitzvah, he'd be called up to the Torah by his Hebrew name. Nachman Dovid would become a Bar Mitzvah this time openly and in freedom.

Noah knew he couldn't choose to have a Bar Mitzvah for the sake of his great-grandfather, a man he'd never met. If he chose to do this, it had to be for himself.

But Nathan's story did have something to do with Noah's decision finally to have a Bar Mitzvah. Noah was named in honor of Nathan. Wouldn't he be dishonoring Nathan to just throw away the opportunity to have a Bar Mitzvah after what Nathan went through to have his? The Jewish traditions were important to Noah. Could he really not continue this major tradition and feel okay about it?

No, he decided. He was Jewish and having a Bar Mitzvah was an important part of being Jewish.

He would not feel right if he did not become Bar Mitzvah, did not take part in this tradition that linked him to his ancestors. He would have a Bar Mitzvah because it was part of who he was, part of his culture and heritage.

When he told his parents his decision, he was surprised by their reaction. He expected his mother to be thrilled. He thought his father wouldn't be too happy since he'd hated his own Bar Mitzvah so much. Noah brought up the subject at dinner one night.

"Mom, Dad. There's something I want to talk to you about."

"Sure, buddy. What's up?" said Dad.

"I've decided I want to have a Bar Mitzvah," said Noah. He waited, surprised by the silence that followed.

"Mom?"

"This is so sudden, Noah. You haven't said anything about a Bar Mitzvah since you quit Hebrew school in third grade. What brought this on?" asked Mom.

"Well, Dan and Aaron started talking about their Bar Mitzvahs and all my friends were asking me if I was having one. So I started thinking about it."

"Did you think about how much work it will be? Dan and Aaron go to Hebrew school. They can read Hebrew and have probably already learned most of the prayers and blessings. You'd have to learn to

read Hebrew before you could begin Bar Mitzvah lessons."

"Gee, Mom, I thought you'd be happy that I want to do this," said Noah.

"Well, I am," said Mom cautiously. "But it is a lot of work. You have to want to do this for the right reasons and you have to make a commitment to study. Why do you want to have a Bar Mitzvah?"

"Because I'm Jewish and it's part of our tradition. Our traditions are important to me and I think I'll feel weird if I'm the only boy in our family not to have a Bar Mitzvah. Zaydie told me how his father had to have a secret Bar Mitzvah in Russia because Jews weren't allowed to practice their religion. It seems almost selfish of me not to have a Bar Mitzvah when my great-grandfather struggled to have one, and I can just have one in front of the whole world."

Mom and Dad just looked at each other for a minute. Then Dad said, "Noah, I'm really proud of you. That's a very mature answer. You've obviously given this a lot of thought, and I respect your decision."

"Yes," said Mom. "I'm very impressed with what you said. But I just want to be sure that you're being honest with yourself as well as with us and you aren't just doing this because your friends are, or because you want a party and gifts."

"Well," said Noah, "that was the reason at first.

When my friends asked me if I was having a Bar Mitzvah, it felt weird to say no. Especially when Aaron and Dan talked about theirs. I didn't want to be the only Jewish kid not to have one. And yeah, I like the idea of a party and gifts. But I knew those weren't good enough reasons. It's mostly because it's part of our tradition."

"Okay," said Mom. "You have to do this for the right reasons because it will be a lot of work for me as well as for you. Besides planning the ceremony and the party, I'll have to teach you Hebrew and help you practice."

"Oh, no you won't, Mom. Zaydie will."

"Zaydie will?"

"Yeah. We talked about it when I quit Hebrew school. He said if I decided to have a Bar Mitzvah, he'd teach me Hebrew and help me learn all the blessings and stuff."

"Oh," said Mom. Noah thought she looked kind of sad. Then she asked, "Have you talked to Zaydie about this yet?"

"No," said Noah. "I wanted to talk to you guys first."

"Well, Noah," said Mom. "It sounds like you've made up your mind. Just realize that once you make this commitment, you'll have to study and practice every day with no complaining. And once we start the planning, you'll have to go through with it.

You can't change your mind. That's why I say that although I certainly understand that the party and the fact that your friends are having Bar Mitzvahs are part of your reason for wanting to have one, those reasons aren't enough. You really have to want to do this."

"I do, Mom. But how much Hebrew do you think I'll have to read?"

"I don't know, Noah. All of the prayers and blessings are in Hebrew. And, of course, when you read from the Torah, it's in Hebrew. We should meet with the rabbi. He can show you how much you'll have to learn. Should I make an appointment?"

"Yeah, I guess so," said Noah hesitantly. "But will I have enough time? I'll be thirteen in two months."

"You don't have to have your Bar Mitzvah right when you turn thirteen. We'll take as much time as you need to prepare. We'll talk to the rabbi and then you can make your final decision, okay? And if you're sure you want to do this, I'll help you. I'm very proud of you, Noah."

They met with the rabbi the following week. Afterward, Noah went to see Zaydie.

"Zaydie, I have something for you," said Noah.

"What's this?" asked Zaydie, when Noah handed him a book.

"It's the book they use in Hebrew school to teach kids Hebrew," said Noah. "The rabbi gave

it to me."

"The rabbi gave it to you? Why?"

"So you can teach me Hebrew. I'm having a Bar Mitzvah."

Noah grinned as he watched the various expressions that crossed Zaydie's face. First, he looked confused. Then, when Noah said he was having a Bar Mitzvah, Zaydie's face went blank for a minute. As he realized what Noah said, a smile spread slowly across Zaydie's face until he was beaming. Noah had never seen Zaydie look so happy or so proud.

"Really? But you never said anything to me about it. Don't we always tell each other everything? Why didn't you tell me you were thinking about this?" asked Zaydie, still beaming.

"Well, actually," said Noah, "I did ask you questions about learning Hebrew and stuff. I just didn't tell you why I was asking. I didn't want to say anything until I was sure. I didn't want to disappoint you again."

"Again? When did you ever disappoint me?"

"When I quit Hebrew school and told you that I didn't want to have a Bar Mitzvah."

"Oh, Noah, you could never disappoint me. I've always been so proud of you. You and I have a special bond, always have. When you were a tiny baby, you cried all the time. I was the only one who seemed to be able to soothe you. I'd put you over my

shoulder and we'd sit in the rocking chair and I'd read to you. I'd just read whatever book I was in the middle of and you'd stop crying. I swear you were listening to the story. I think you cried so much just to get me to read to you."

"Zaydie, I was just a baby."

"Well, maybe you just liked hearing my voice. But ever since then we've been pals, right?"

"Right. So, Zaydie, do you think it will be hard for me to learn Hebrew?"

"No. Since you were a little boy you've always accomplished anything you decided to do. It will be a lot of work, but that's never stopped you before."

Noah gave Zaydie a big hug. "I'm glad you'll be helping me. I'm kind of nervous about doing this."

"Don't worry. You can do this. Together we'll do it and it'll be fun. I'll come over every day after school. We'll learn a letter a day."

Zaydie was right. Learning to read Hebrew wasn't that hard, but it was a lot of work. Some of the Hebrew letters were easy to recognize, but some of them looked a lot like other letters. And then there were the vowels. They weren't actual letters like in English. They were marks that appeared under or next to the letters. Noah couldn't believe it when Zaydie told him that the Torah is written without any vowels.

"What?" exclaimed Noah. "How will I be able to read it?"

"The copy you'll learn from will have the vowels," said Zaydie. "You'll know the words well enough to be able to read them without vowels by the time of your Bar Mitzvah."

Because they practiced almost every day, Noah learned to read Hebrew in about six weeks. His mother got in touch with a Bar Mitzvah tutor, Beth, and arranged a schedule for lessons. Noah would start in two weeks and go every Sunday afternoon for six months. Each lesson was only half an hour long. Beth would teach him the blessings, songs, and prayers for the service. Then she'd teach him small sections of his Torah portion and Haftorah reading. He would have to practice during the week to learn what she taught him each Sunday. But he hadn't worried about that. Zaydie was going to help him.

But now, it was just days before his first Bar Mitzvah lesson with Beth, and Noah was lying on his bed, crying. Zaydie was dead. Noah was devastated. It made no sense. How could it be true he'd never see Zaydie again? Where was Zaydie now? Not his body, but Zaydie himself. Could he feel Noah's pain? Did he know that Noah missed him already?

The next day, Mom and Bubbie went to the funeral home to make arrangements. Dad stayed home with Noah, but Noah just wanted to be alone. He stayed in his room all day, channel-surfing on the TV but not really watching anything. Occasionally,

something would catch his attention for a few minutes, but then he'd remember Zaydie was dead, and it was like finding out all over again. Each time he remembered, the shock and the pain were as bad as when Mom had told him yesterday. Noah didn't think this kind of pain could ever go away.

When Mom came home, Noah heard her talking quietly to Dad downstairs for a while. Then they both came up to his room.

"Noah?" Mom knocked on his door.

"Come in," said Noah in a soft voice. His head was stuffed up from crying, and his voice was hoarse and strained.

"I thought you'd like to know about the funeral," said Mom as she sat down on Noah's bed. "It's tomorrow at the synagogue. After that we'll go the cemetery, and then everyone will go to Bubbie's house."

When Noah didn't say anything, Dad said, "Noah, do you have any questions?"

Noah hesitated, and then asked, "Do I have to go?"

"You mean to Bubbie's house?" asked Mom.

"Do I have to go the funeral?" asked Noah, not looking at anyone.

No one spoke for a moment, then Mom said, "Well, I guess it's up to you. I assumed you'd go. You're old enough. But this will be your first funeral, and I'm sorry it has to be for someone you loved so

much. It will be hard for you, for all of us."

Noah didn't say anything. Mom continued, "It's a mitzvah to attend a funeral, to honor the person who's died. It's a way for you to show your respect for the person. It also helps you realize the person is really gone. And I think you will feel better if you help lay Zaydie to rest. It will give you a chance to say good-bye."

When Noah finally looked at Mom, his eyes were wide with fright. "Will I have to see him?" he asked.

"Oh, no, Noah," Mom said, putting her arms around him. "No, you won't see him. Sometimes at funerals in other religions, the coffin is open. But Jews keep the coffin closed so that we can remember the person in life, not in death."

Noah relaxed at little. "Okay. I'll go. I want to be there for Zaydie." Noah's voice broke as he said, 'Zaydie,' and he started to cry.

"I miss him so much already," he sobbed into his mother's shoulder. "I can't believe I'll never see him again."

Dad came over and sat on the bed, and he and Mom hugged Noah tightly.

The next day when they got to the synagogue, the coffin was already there in front of the *bimah*. The coffin was covered with a cloth and someone was sitting next to it, praying. Mom had explained that

according to Jewish tradition, the body is never left alone from the moment of death until burial. Noah liked the idea that someone was keeping Zaydie company.

When Noah hugged Bubbie, she held him tightly and whispered, "Zaydie loved you so much. You were so special to him."

Noah couldn't say anything. He sat down and tried not to look at the coffin. He couldn't imagine, couldn't believe Zaydie was in there. During the service, Noah kept his eyes on his prayer book. He turned the pages when everyone else did but didn't really see what they were reading. Looking at the Hebrew words was hard. It reminded him of Zaydie. He tried reading some of it and when he found he could, he wanted to say, "Hey, Zaydie, listen to this." But then he remembered. Zaydie couldn't hear him, could he?

The family rode to the cemetery in a limo. Noah had never been in one before and normally would have thought it was cool. But today he barely noticed. He was nervous about going to the cemetery. Mom had told him that after the rabbi said some prayers, the coffin would be lowered into the grave. She also said that the custom was for people to shovel some dirt into the grave to cover the coffin. She said it was a mitzvah, but Noah didn't think he could do that.

It was painful watching the coffin being

lowered into the grave. Bubbie, Mom, and Noah's aunts and uncles each threw a shovelful of dirt in. Suddenly, Noah wanted to help bury Zaydie. He walked up to the dirt pile and picked up a handful of dirt. He stood next to the grave with his eyes closed for a moment. Then he took a deep breath, opened his eyes, and looked down. The coffin was half-covered. Noah held out his fist and slowly sprinkled dirt back and forth over the coffin.

"I'll never forget you, Zaydie," Noah said to himself. "I love you."

His parents were waiting as Noah stepped away from the grave. They both put their arms around him.

Going to Bubbie and Zaydie's house without Zaydie there was awful. The whole thing was weird. It was like a party, but not a party. There were lots of people and lots of food. But everyone was sad and talked quietly at first. After a while people were telling stories about Zaydie. Some stories were funny and people smiled, even laughed. Noah was horrified. How could they laugh when Zaydie was dead?

People even talked about things that had nothing to do with Zaydie. Uncle David came up to Noah and said, "So, Noah. I hear you decided to have a Bar Mitzvah. That's great. What made you change your mind?"

Uncle David had been teasing Noah about this ever since Noah quit Hebrew school. Whenever he saw Noah, he'd make a stupid remark like, "Started studying for you Bar Mitzvah yet?" Or "Picked a date for your Bar Mitzvah yet?" Noah hated it. Did his uncle really think that Noah would change his mind just because he kept mentioning it? Now he probably thought it was because of him that Noah had decided to have a Bar Mitzvah.

All of Noah's feelings suddenly burst out of him and he yelled at Uncle David, "I'm not having a Bar Mitzvah! Not without Zaydie!"

Noah ran down the hall to the small study and slammed the door behind him. He crawled into Zaydie's chair, the one where he always read, and curled up into a ball as small as he could. He held his breath as long as he could, then let it out slowly and waited for his heart to stop pounding.

When he sensed someone standing beside him, he slowly opened his eyes and looked up. Expecting, hoping, to see Zaydie, he was surprised to see Bubbie. She smiled sadly and sat down beside him. She said, "I have something for you, Noah."

She handed him a small, faded blue velvet bag. There was a Jewish star embroidered on it. "Open it," said Bubbie.

Noah unzipped the bag and looked inside. When he didn't say anything, Bubbie said, "Take it out."

Noah pulled some old fabric gently out of the bag. When he still didn't say anything, Bubbie asked him, "Do you know what it is?"

"It's a *tallit*," said Noah quietly. "A prayer shawl to wear in synagogue."

"It's not just any tallit," said Bubbie. "It's Zaydie's tallit. He was planning to give it to you to wear at your Bar Mitzvah. Before it was Zaydie's, it was his father Nathan's. Nathan wore it at his own Bar Mitzvah."

"You mean the secret Bar Mitzvah in Russia?" asked Noah.

"Yes. The secret Bar Mitzvah. When Zaydie had his Bar Mitzvah, Nathan was so thrilled to be able to celebrate his son's Bar Mitzvah without hiding, he gave his tallit to Zaydie to wear. He wanted his tallit to cover a Bar Mitzvah in freedom. And Zaydie wanted you to wear the same tallit that he and his father wore.

He liked the idea of this tallit escaping from oppression and celebrating many Bar Mitzvahs in freedom. He hoped that one day you might pass it on to your son and his son, and on and on. I don't know when he was planning to give this to you, but I think today is the right time."

Noah hugged the tallit to his chest and said tearfully, "I don't think I can have a Bar Mitzvah without Zaydie."

"You won't be without him," said Bubbie.

169

"You'll wear his tallit and he'll be hugging you. He'll be there with you, believe me."

"But who'll help me study?" Noah asked in a trembling voice.

"I will," said Mom. She had come in so quietly, Noah didn't realize she was there. "I didn't go to Hebrew school five days a week for nothing. I can read Hebrew and I know all the prayers. I'll help you, Noah, if you decide you still want to do this. It's still your choice, and you still need to want to do this for yourself. Not for anyone else."

Noah slowly wrapped the tallit around his shoulders. It was so old and soft, and it smelled like… like Zaydie. It smelled like Zaydie's aftershave lotion. Suddenly Noah could hear Zaydie's voice saying, "Noah, you could never disappoint me. I've always been so proud of you. You've always accomplished anything you decided to do."

"I decided," Noah said out loud, surprising himself as well as Mom and Bubbie.

"What?" asked Mom.

"I already decided to have a Bar Mitzvah, and I always accomplish what I decide to do. So I'll do it."

Noah wrapped the tallit more tightly around him and thought, *and Zaydie will be right there with me.*

GROUP LABOR

By Tiferet Peterseil

171

Tiferet Peterseil

I am a graphic designer at Simcha Publishing Company and a gymnastics instructor at "Kvitz-Kvotz," in Jerusalem, Israel.

Although I works in many fields, my ambition is to become a professional actress.

Since my first nephew was born, I began to pay closer attention to expectant mothers and their family relationships and discovered that there was nothing more amazing and amusing.

There is also nothing more real.

I feel anyone who has had a newborn child, niece or nephew, sibling, or even a friend, can relate to Group Labor at some level.

Because everyone knows, that behind every happy pregnant woman, are her family and friends.

GROUP LABOR

I suppose my first clue was when Uncle Aryeh came to visit us in Israel.

"Congratulations!" he said, hugging me.

"Congratulations? On what?" I asked.

"On what?" he repeated, seeming confused. "Uh, nothing."

Another sign I should have noticed was Mom fussing over all our old clothes, and Dad suddenly hanging up a picture of our family tree.

But I'm getting ahead of myself. My name is Leah and I'm 17, the third of four children. Most people who hear that I'm a middle child just nod and say, "Ah… that explains a lot."

Raychel (or Raychee) is my 12-year-old sister whose life goal is to annoy me.

Nathan is my 21-year-old brother. He keeps saying he'll get his own apartment, but never seems to actually do it.

Last, but certainly not least, is Bayla (or BeeBee – BB as we like to call her) my 23-year-old sister. BB has been married for over a year now, and lives in the house next door.

BB and I have always had a special relationship. We've always been close and shared all our

secrets. Even when BB got engaged, I knew before our parents did.

Speaking of which, my Mom, a social worker to the core, was worried BB and I would drift apart once she was married. Mom insisted we choose one day a week to get together. "It's important you maintain a strong sisterly bond," she insisted.

So that's how *Sunday-Bonday* began. Ever since BB got married, she and I meet Sunday mornings. I help her shop for whatever she needs, then we go out to lunch.

It's all a routine. Nothing too exciting.

But there's this one Sunday I will never forget:

MONTH ONE – Breaking The News

"What are you going to order?" BB asked me.

It was Sunday-Bonday. BB and I had finished shopping and we were catching a bite to eat at our favorite restaurant.

"The usual," I answered, "and a coke. How about you?" I tried not to meet my sister's eyes.

It was embarrassing; every time I looked at her, she would start giggling.

See, there's something you have to understand about BB. She is the most predictable person in the world. Especially to me. She's never too hot, never too cold. Never that angry, never that excited. She always orders the same food, buys the same cereal, and wears the same colors – gray and brown.

But this morning, my ordinary, predictable, never-too-excited sister, was giggling. I couldn't figure out what had gotten into her. She never giggles.

"I'll stick with the tuna melt," BB turned to the waiter. "A tuna melt, and the omelet special for my sister. Two cokes."

The waiter nodded and scurried off.

I looked at her. She was smiling again and her whole face was glowing with happiness. Something was up, or else she REALLY liked tuna melt.

"So," I cleared my throat, "What's new?"

BB's expression turned serious, and then she smiled again.

"Well Leah... the truth is, I'm not supposed to tell anyone yet. But I just hate keeping it a secret from you anymore. I'm dying to tell someone."

Ah, so something was up. My sister-sensor was working.

"Tell someone what?" I asked innocently.

Her smile grew wider. "I'm pregnant."

"You're what?" My dimples almost popped out of my cheeks!

She giggled, "Pregnant."

I couldn't believe it! "Wow, that's great, BB! Pregnant! My own sister."

Then it dawned on me – "Oh my God! Does Joe know?"

"Of course! He was the first to know."

175

"Right." I suppose it made sense. He *should* know before me. They *are* a married couple. I mean, Joe would've noticed when an infant started crying in the spare bedroom.

"So you haven't told anyone?" I asked.

That's a silly question. Of course she hadn't! I'm *always* the first to know.

"Um, not really," BB replied.

Not really? What did that mean?

"How about Mom and Dad? Do they know?" I asked.

"Yes, we told them."

Well, that made sense too, I guess. I could let that pass.

"And Joe's parents?" I inquired further.

"Yes, we told them too."

They are also the grandparents, so that makes sense, too. Okay, I was still one of the first to know.

"So that's it," I concluded.

"Almost," BB winced a little.

"Almost? Well, who else knows?"

"Aunt Dorothy called," BB explained. "She asked what was new. And you know me – I *can't* lie. Once I told her, I had to tell all the other aunts and uncles so no one would be insulted."

"That explains Uncle Aryeh. He wished me congratulations," I said. "Who else did you tell?"

"That's it! Honest! Just the aunts and uncles!"

"What about Grandma?" I interrogated.

"Oh yes. Yes, I did tell her. But that's it!" BB said.

"And Cousin Iris?"

"Oh, right."

I didn't like where this was heading.

"How about your best friend Naomi? And Sarah?"

"Yes. Them too..." BB said sheepishly.

"What about Yaara, our neighbor?"

"Yeah, I sort of slipped up there."

I was throwing my last lifeline out. My dignity was on the line now.

"Does Raychee know?"

A pause – "Uh, but I just told her today."

My younger sister knew before me! This was horrific!

"So, I'm more like the last one to know?"

"Well, maybe," BB said, embarrassed. "But it's a secret. Don't tell anyone!"

My sister couldn't keep a secret if her life depended on it! I wouldn't be surprised if my *own* friends knew. I guess it *is* sort of a hard secret to keep for too long. I suppose I *could* let it pass. "How far along are you?" I asked.

"A month."

A MONTH?! In ONE month she managed to tell half of Jerusalem?

"Oooh, that's really just the beginning of your pregnancy," I said, trying to drop a subtle hint.

"Yeah, it is." She didn't get it.

Okay, let's put things into perspective, I told myself. So there's ONE thing I wasn't the first to know about. It happens. It doesn't make us less close.

"How do you feel?" I inquired, trying to sound as sisterly as possible.

"Just fine," she smiled. "I don't know what all these pregnant women complain about. It's a piece of cake. I'm as happy as could be!"

Yes, I remember that Sunday. The Sunday when BB told me she was pregnant. She was so happy. Positively glowing. So looking forward to the next eight months. So sure it was all going to be a blast.

Poor thing.

She didn't know what hit her.

MONTH TWO - Morning Sickness

"My head hurts," BB complained.

"Let's stop here and get you a cold drink," I suggested.

Sunday-Bonday again. We had barely accomplished any shopping.

I approached the vendor. "A coke please."

"No, not a coke. I'll drink orange juice," my sister corrected.

"Orange juice? Since when?" BB *never* drank

orange juice.

"Since I started reading the baby book," BB explained. "It says no caffeine or bubbles during pregnancy. Bad for the baby."

"What?" I said, paying the vendor. "What is this book called?"

"*World War Three In Your Stomach.*"

Was she joking? I couldn't tell. "Are you kidding?"

"No. That's the name of the book."

Boy, where does she find these things? Leave it to BB.

"Well," I teased, "I wouldn't trust a book with a title like that."

BB drank her juice.

"Gee, this headache just won't leave me alone."

"Did you have breakfast?" I asked.

"No."

"So let's have an early lunch."

At our usual restaurant, we ordered...the usual.

"I'm so nauseous," BB gagged.

"You'll feel better once you eat."

Hey, I'm 17. What did I know?

"Yeah," BB sighed. But then her expression changed. "Uh-oh! I don't feel so good!"

She put her hands to her mouth and dashed into the bathroom. When BB finally came back, our food had come.

"You okay?" I asked, concerned.

"Yes," BB replied, sipping from her water. "It's just that the morning sickness started coming in the afternoons and evenings as well. Ooh, the tuna looks good." Her eyes lit up as she took a bite out of it.

"Oh no!" BB clasped her hands to her mouth and ran back to the bathroom.

I looked down at my omelet. It suddenly didn't seem as appealing as usual with my sister's gagging sounds filtering in from the bathroom.

BB returned, looking a touch green.

"There, I think I feel better now." She took another bite out of her sandwich.

Well, if she can eat, then I really should too.

The eggs had just reached my lips, when BB cried out, "Oh no!" and ran to the bathroom again.

She stayed there a long time, and my omelet grew colder and even less appetizing.

When BB finally did return, I offered her some of my omelet. I thought maybe it was just the tuna that made her feel sick. She looked at me, and ran back into the bathroom.

I waited. And waited. My stomach was grumbling. I was definitely hungry. All right, I thought to myself, I should try to eat the omelet before it gets too cold. But every time I took a forkful, I remembered BB's expression and became nauseous myself. This was ridiculous. I wasn't the pregnant one, I thought to myself. I looked at my rebellious omelet

and took a bite. It tasted pretty good. I managed to eat quite a bit by the time BB rejoined me, looking greener than ever.

"Sorry about that, Leah," she apologized. "But I think it's safe to say I won't be sharing your eggs. Thanks anyway."

"Don't worry about it," I comforted her. "It just means more omelet for me!"

Judging from the look that came over her, I thought she might throw up again. Finally, she smiled and said, "I think I'm going to give up on lunch."

That was my cue. "Yeah? Okay, I'll ask them to wrap up the leftovers."

BB tapped my hand gently. "Don't be silly. Eat. Really."

It didn't seem right eating by myself. Besides, what if she got sick just watching me eat? I'd feel terrible. On the other hand, my stomach was making awful noises.

"Are you sure?" I asked her.

"Yes, of course," she said, nodding.

"Okay." I took another bite out of my omelet.

BB watched me and smiled. She seemed okay. But when I went for the second bite, it was all over. BB was gagging in the bathroom and I had absolutely, positively lost my appetite.

MONTH THREE – Mood Swings

BB was constantly tired. When our usual Sunday-Bonday came, she now preferred that I come to her house. She said she just didn't have the strength to move.

I only got to her house at around 11:00 A.M., but she was still in her pajamas. Her hair was a mess, and her eyes were all red.

"What's the matter?" I asked. "Didn't you get any sleep last night?"

"No," she replied, miserable. "I had nightmares."

"Nightmares?" I repeated. "What kind of nightmares?"

"I dreamed I had the baby. But I kept forgetting to feed it. It was terrible!"

"Oh, don't worry," I consoled her. "You're going to be a great mom!"

"No, I'm not! I'm going to be a terrible mother!"

I guess she woke up on the wrong side of the bed.

"BB, trust me," I patted her shoulder. "You are a great sister to me, a great daughter to Mom and Dad, and a great wife to Joe. I don't have a doubt in my mind you will be a wonderful mother to your child."

BB still appeared annoyed.

"Are you hungry?" I tried to change the subject. "Can I fix us some lunch?"

"Yes. Of course I'm hungry," BB snapped. "All I do is throw up, and when I'm not doing that I'm stuffing four tons of food down my throat. I'm eating so much I'm afraid there may not be any room left for the baby!"

She was so angry her face had turned red. I wasn't sure what to do.

"Let's eat cereal," she mumbled.

"Okay." I brought what we needed to the table.

"So what's new?" BB asked, suddenly calm.

"Not much, since I last spoke with you," I said. "But I finally hung up that poster you bought me."

"The one I got you for your birthday? That was ages ago. You finally hung it up?" BB asked.

"Yep. That's the one," I agreed. "Hey, didn't you have an ultrasound Friday morning?"

"Yeah," she said, very focused on her food. "It was amazing. The baby is so tiny."

BB made a tower of seven cheerios on her spoon. I know, because by the time she managed to get them lined up, I had counted them, twice!

"How about the heartbeat? Did you hear it?" I asked.

"Yjub. Bjut Ij Donzt Junder – " BB said, crunching a mouth full of cereal.

"Whoa, whoa. I don't understand what you're saying."

She swallowed and then worked on beating her

record. I could tell she was going to go for ten.

"Yes," BB repeated. "I heard the heartbeat. But I don't understand how it could be beating so fast!" Nine cheerios were piled high, as she carefully placed the tenth on top. She opened wide and, "CRUNCH", gobbled them up.

We talked a bit more. After that I'm not sure what happened, but somehow BB managed to spill her second bowl of cereal all over the place.

"Great! Just great!" BB yelled, jumping out of her chair. "Now I'm all wet! And everything is sticky and dirty! Wonderful!"

"Here, I'll get that." I grabbed a towel off the counter and started mopping the floor.

"No! That's the Shabbat towel!" BB grabbed it out of my hand. I don't remember ever seeing her so angry.

"Just… just…. Just let me do it alone! Being pregnant doesn't mean I can't do anything by myself anymore!"

I backed away, a little startled. I finished my breakfast uncomfortably and watched while BB cleaned up.

"So how are you feeling in general?" I asked BB, as we washed the dishes.

"Terrible!" she snapped. "I don't have patience for anything and I'm too tired to think straight!"

"I would never have guessed," I said, with a wink.

I didn't want the rest of our day to continue this way. I figured we couldn't go wrong watching a movie. It didn't demand much concentration.

I suggested going to the video store together. BB liked the idea of watching a movie but said she felt too tired and bloated to move. So I ran down to the video store by myself. I rented three movies. When I got back to the house I presented them to BB. She had seen two of them. The third she hadn't seen but made a point of telling me it didn't look good.

"Should I go and exchange it?" I offered.

"No, forget it. Let's just watch," she replied grumpily.

I made some popcorn and we started the movie.

"This really looks bad!" BB repeated.

"BB! I told you I don't mind switching it!" My patience was wearing thin.

"And I told you I don't mind watching it!" BB retorted.

"So are we watching it?"

"Yes!"

"Fine," and I added quietly. "Don't have a cow!"

"What?" BB strained to hear what I was saying.

"Nothing."

Her angry eyes focused on the television screen. I realized I had better keep my cool. After

all, she *was* pregnant.

I tried to start a conversation. "BB, I don't understand. Did the guy running take it, or didn't he?"

"How should I know! I never saw this movie!" BB shouted.

"I was just ask – "

"Just watch!" she commanded.

Ouch! It was too early in the day to get my head chopped off!

I didn't look at her throughout the movie. When it ended, I saw she had fallen asleep. Poor BB. My heart went out to her. I brought a blanket to cover her. But when I did, she woke up.

"Until I finally get a little sleep!" BB snapped, grabbed the blanket from my hand, and went back to sleep.

I stared at her in disbelief.

Nice going, Mom, I thought. *You just had to come up with stupid Sunday-Bonday!*

MONTH FOUR – Gaining weight

I'm not sure if BB stopped being so grouchy, or if I just got used to it. But even when she did throw a fit, I just let it pass and forced myself not to take it to heart.

Raychee, on the other hand, was not handling this pregnancy experience as well as I was.

Nathan had finally found an apartment and

we were helping him move into it.

"I still can't believe he went through with it," Mom shook her head in dismay. "I mean, as it is he's barely ever home. I wonder if we'll see him *at all* now that he's gone."

"Mom, he's not dead, he just moved," I said. I could tell Mom was worried about our 'bonding' situation.

Raychee was climbing the steps with a heavy box, three bags hanging from her arms, and two blankets flung over her shoulders. She could barely see the steps. "Why shouldn't he want to move?" she mumbled through the blankets. "I would too, if I had a bunch of slaves carrying my stuff for me!"

Dad was going down to the car when he saw BB had picked up two pots.

"Hold on," Dad shouted, taking the pots from BB. "Not you! You don't carry anything."

"But I feel like I have to do *something*!" BB insisted.

Dad looked around and spotted Raychee. "Here," he said, taking one of the bags from her. It was an empty knapsack. "Carry this up." He handed it to BB and put the pots on top of the blankets Raychee was carrying.

"Wonderful!" Raychee complained. "Why don't we just load the whole car on me and give BB Nathan's toothbrush to carry!"

Luckily, no one heard her but me. "I'll help you," I offered.

"No thanks. Don't you know I'm an ant? I seem to be able to carry ten times my weight!" Raychee called as she climbed up the remaining stairs.

Wow! Is pregnancy contagious or what?

Dad decided BB would be the most "helpful" if she stayed near the car and helped organize who would carry what.

BB did a good job but most of the time she was running up and down the stairs to the bathroom.

Nothing gets past my Mom, and she noticed how distressed Raychee seemed to be.

"You know, girls," Mom said, on the way back home. "I know Raychee has been wanting to get some shirts she saw downtown."

I looked at Raychee. Her hands were folded across her chest and she was staring angrily out the car window.

Mom turned to her, "Why don't you go shopping with Leah and BB tomorrow? I'll even give BB the car so you can drive there."

That's probably what convinced Raychee. She loves to be driven. "Practice for when I get a chauffeur," she would say. She's so lazy, I wouldn't be surprised if she bought a scooter so she could ride to her room instead of taking the four steps to get there.

In the mall the following day, Raychee was like a clothes addict on a shopping spree. Which she was.

"Oooh, look at this!" Raychee squealed with delight, running from one display window to the next. "Oh, and this shirt! Isn't it amazing? Did you ever see a shirt with a picture of a skirt on it? Isn't that creative? That's like two in one!"

Raychee couldn't stop moving for a second. BB was getting out of breath, so I bought some ice cream for BB and me. We ate while Raychee tried on clothes.

Raychee came out of the dressing room wearing a shirt four sizes too small for her. It was so tight her ribs were showing.

"Wow!" BB sighed, taking another lick of her ice cream. "Raychee, you are so skinny!"

That really made Raychee's day. "So are you, BB," she replied graciously, disappearing into the dressing room.

"No, I'm not." BB looked at her ice cream cone. Then at mine. BB had almost finished hers while I was just beginning. "I'm fat!"

"BB!" I said. "You're being ridiculous! We can barely tell you're pregnant!"

"No, I'm all fat. I feel fat," she whined. "I eat like a pig and look like a cow!"

"Well, we all eat like pigs," Raychee declared. She came out of the dressing room wearing a striped green T-shirt. "But as long as you don't start snorting, I wouldn't worry just yet."

BB turned to me. "I hate this." She plopped the last bit of cone into her mouth. "I am so fat. I can barely move." She shrugged. "Oh well, I have to go."

And she went to the bathroom.

"Look Raychee, I'm not saying it's easy, but you're going to have to be more patient and well... *sweeter* about this whole pregnancy thing."

It was close to midnight. Raychee and I were in her room, and had been talking for over an hour.

"I'm very sweet!" she snapped.

Sure, I thought, *sweet as pie, that one*.

"Girls," Moms' sleepy voice echoed in as she cracked open the door. "What are you doing up?"

"Sorry, Mom. Were we too loud?" I asked.

"That's okay," Mom smiled and sat on the bed with us. "I was only half sleeping anyway. I was thinking about BB."

"That's just what we were talking about," Raychee pouted. "BB is taking up everyone's attention and is always upset about something or other. And if not that, then she's eating these weird foods and then complaining about getting fat!"

Mom laughed. I was glad she was taking it that way and not yelling at Raychee for being so insensitive.

"Honey," Mom began, "if you think it's hard

for us, think how hard it must be for BB. Suddenly everything has changed for her. She's always hungry, and always grumpy. She's not happy with the way she looks and she always feels terrible. That's why we have to be as sympathetic as we can. Pregnancy is not easy. Believe me, I've been through it four times!"

Wow. How did Mom do that?

"Well," I said, glancing at the unhappy Raychee, "Mom, I hope you feel it was worth it."

"Of course it was!" Mom hugged me. "Nine months is nothing compared to a lifetime. And when you have the love and support of a family, the nine months aren't all that hard."

I thought about that. All in all, I was more than happy to be there for BB. But it did take a lot out of me.

"Mom, when you were pregnant, was it hard on Dad?" I asked.

"Oh, I'm sure! I'm sure it's quite tough on Joe, too. He has been very uptight lately, and I know he feels guilty not being home for BB all the time. I think he is very grateful that we are here. Do you know, when I was pregnant with you, Leah, Dad had what is called 'sympathy pains.'"

"What's that?" Raychee asked.

"Well, Dad was so involved and concerned with my pregnancy, that he felt some of the things I did.

He was hungry every time I was, and his back ached whenever mine did. It was pretty funny, actually," Mom explained. "See, that sometimes happens to the people who are close to the woman who's pregnant."

Raychee laughed, "Thank God that hasn't happened to us!"

"You never know," Mom winked and kissed Raychee goodnight. I wished Raychee sweet dreams and stepped into the hall with Mom.

"Alright Leah. We'd better get to bed." Mom hugged me.

"Mom?" I asked. "Do you think BB and I will still be close after she has the baby?"

Mom smiled. "I think you'll discover you are even closer."

"Yeah, right! Even closer? We're about a mile apart right now...," I said sadly. "BB is in a different world than I am! She... she... she's like a different person. I don't really know how to talk to her anymore...."

Mom listened carefully and then said, "Leah, try talking about this with BB. I think you'll feel better once you do."

I thought about it. Could BB understand? Would she be upset? Would she feel bad? "Okay, thanks Mom," I finally said and wished her goodnight.

Next chance I got, I would try to talk with BB. That is, if she didn't bite my head off first!

MONTH FIVE - Cravings

BB started showing. Her face
and hands were getting swollen, and it
was a rare sight to see her without food in
her hands or far from a bathroom.

Our *Sunday-Bonday* sort of faded out because
BB was at our house all the time and then, once Joe
got back from work, she would rush back to her house.
I enjoyed seeing so much of BB.

We had finished lunch just an hour before and
there she was, sitting at the kitchen table with an
assortment of spreads and jellies laid out in front of
her. But what occupied all her attention at the moment was the way she was carefully spreading mayonnaise onto her biscuit. Bellvis, our huge dog, was
sitting and drooling beside her.

"BB? Is that mayonnaise on your biscuit?" I
asked, sitting down near her.

"Oh, yes. You should try it, it's delicious." She
took another bite. "You know, I didn't appreciate food
enough before I was pregnant. I mean, take jelly and
sauerkraut, for example. I never thought that would
work. But you know what? It's amazing. Tastes heavenly. You should try it!"

"No, thanks," I said, taking a biscuit. "I think
I'll stick with *plain* biscuits."

Was this the right time to speak to her? Should
I get it all out in the open?

"Your loss, Leah," BB declared. "It's not too

late for you! You can still learn how to eat all the delicious foods that I've missed out on all these ye – Hey! YOUR DOG JUST ATE MY BISCUIT!"

It was true. Bellvis had simply grabbed it out of BB's hand, and was now happily licking his lips. This was definitely not the time for a "serious" talk. The loss of food was nothing short of a *disaster* for BB.

"He did?" I laughed. "I guess dogs really *do* eat everything."

Raychee walked into the kitchen. "You should talk," she mumbled, pouring herself a glass of juice and joining us at the table.

"What's that supposed to mean?" I asked angrily. "Are you implying something?"

"I'm not implying anything," Raychee answered. "I'm saying very clearly that you have the appetite of a goat. You eat everything, including your nails."

"Euw! I don't eat them. I bite them!" I corrected, taking another bite out of my biscuit.

BB started spreading some cream cheese and peanut butter onto another biscuit. "I think you don't feed your dog enough. He's always after my food."

Oh shoot! That's what I forgot to do this morning! Feed the dog! But I couldn't let them know that, so I said indignantly: "Of course I feed him."

I made a note to myself to feed the dog first chance I got.

"Maybe he's pregnant too," Raychee teased, nauseated by the combination of spreads BB had chosen.

"Or, maybe he's just trying to get some attention." I went over to pat the dog. "Wis my Wittwle Bellvis twying to get some atttttention?" I cooed, feeding him the remainder of my biscuit. After watching BB, I couldn't possibly eat anymore. And besides, I thought I should feed him anything I could until I could slip him his dog food.

BB looked at me, revolted. She didn't care much for the dog and couldn't stand when I talked to him in what she calls a baby voice. "What kind of name is Bellvis for a dog anyway?"

"Don't ask me," I shrugged. "Raychee chose it. I think that's why none of the other dogs will play with him."

"I did not choose Bellvis! I chose Belle!" Raychee explained. "And *then* you discovered she was a boy and changed his name to Bellvis! *I* still call him Belle for short."

"I know," I grunted. "He's got a complex from it. He doesn't have a clue what his name is. Watch. He'll answer to any name."

I took a step back.

"Come here, notebook," I called. The dog happily trotted over to me. "See!"

BB smiled. "Come here, stupid," she called,

and the dog came. "Boy, this dog has issues. Uh-oh, I gotta go again."

BB went to the bathroom.

"I don't understand how she could eat this stuff?" Raychee said, picking up a jar of horseradish. "I mean, doesn't she have tastebuds?"

"It's called *cravings*," I informed her. "Mom said pregnant women get this way."

"Hey!" BB yelled as she came back into the kitchen. "Your dog ate my biscuit again!"

"No he didn't," I jumped to his defense. "I was watching. He didn't jump onto the table!"

"It wasn't on the table!" BB whined. "It was on the floor."

"What was it doing on the floor?" Raychee asked, puzzled.

"I accidentally dropped it on my way to the bathroom. I was going to pick it up on my way back." BB sulked into a chair. "Look, I'm so fat, I have to plan ahead of time when I'm going to bend over!"

I giggled and grabbed a biscuit. "You're not fat, BB. You're carrying a baby in there. Here, I'll make you another one."

I started smearing some cream cheese onto the biscuit.

"Ugh," Raychee whined.

"Stop it, Raychee," I ordered. "BB? How much cream cheese should I put on?"

"More," BB instructed. "Yeah, a little more.

Right, now the peanut butter. No. More. More, more... A little more... No, more than that... Yes, more more... No, too much. I need a new one."

I threw the biscuit to Bellvis in frustration, and grabbed a new one. That dumb dog....

MONTH SIX – Sympathy Pains

BB had decided to keep secret whether the baby was a boy or a girl.

"She's carrying like a girl," Mom would say.

"Oh no, it's definitely a boy. I have a good sense for these things," Dad would argue.

Whatever it was, BB was getting big enough to fool us into believing there were twins in there! But no one dared tell her that. As angry as she had been a few months earlier, her mood drastically changed to one of super sensitivity. I mean, when she saw a mother hug a baby, she would start crying. "That's so beautiful," she would sob.

It was Sunday, and BB and I had just finished lunch at the house and were clearing the table.

"Oooh," BB grimaced carrying a plate to the sink. "My ankles are just killing me! I'm not used to carrying all this weight." She patted her belly.

Funny. I don't believe I gained any weight, but my ankles have been hurting too. I tried to ignore it. "Actually, BB, you don't look so well."

"I know... No matter how much I sleep, I'm still so tired. I have this constant feeling of *blah,*" BB sighed.

My thoughts exactly! Last night I got 13 hours of sleep! But I was still tired! No... it was worse than tired... It was this constant feeling of nervousness... anticipation.... I was always thinking about BB and the baby. I was always worried.

"Oh look at this," BB said, referring to a jump rope that Raychee had no doubt left on the counter. "I haven't jumped rope in ages!"

She picked up the jump rope.

"Well, do you really think now is the right time to start?" I asked. "I mean, you're pregnant! What if you just bounce the baby right out!"

"Nonsense!" BB waved me off. "The book says I can continue doing all the things I used to do before I was pregnant, and I certainly used to jump rope! I used to be so active...."

She put herself into a jumping position. No matter what the book said, I didn't like the idea of her jumping with that potbelly. I crouched low with my hands out.

"What are you doing, Leah?" BB asked.

"Just in case, I'll be ready to catch the baby if it falls out," I told her. She shook her head and started jumping.

"OUCH!" BB cried after the first jump. She looked down at her foot. "My ankle hurts!"

I immediately reached for my ankle. Ow! The second she said that I felt like someone just kicked me. But I breathed a sigh of relief. At least the baby was fine.

"Okay, BB. Let's can the jumping," I said, rubbing my sore ankle. This was strange. I've never had ankle problems. In fact, my ankle only hurts when I'm around BB... Uh-oh. I couldn't possibly be suffering from sympathy pains, could I? No, that's ridiculous. Sympathy pains....

"I guess you're right," she said sadly, putting down the jump rope. "You know, I can't wait until I finally have this baby!"

Right. She'll have the baby and then that'll be the end of our relationship. Maybe I should try talking to her now?

"BB," I began, pulling myself onto the counter, still rubbing my ankle. "I've been wanting to talk – "

"Joey!!" BB suddenly cried out in excitement. I whirled around, and sure enough there was Joe. He came through the front door and walked straight to the kitchen, arms open.

BB melted into them. She was always happy to see him.

"Hi, you," Joe said, hugging BB. "Early day at work. I have the rest of the day off. The truth is, I would've been home earlier but I stopped for some lunch in town."

"Well, at least you ate," BB said. "Joe, I'm so glad you're back. I'm so tired."

Ever since the pregnancy began, BB would wait the whole day for Joe to get back, just so she could complain to him. And he never seemed to mind.

"I'm just so exhausted, Joe."

Me too, I thought.

"And my ankles hurt."

Mine too.

"I think they're swollen, Joe."

BB looked down at her ankles. They were swollen. I looked down at mine. They were swollen too!

"Even my arms hurt."

I suddenly got a painful current through my arms.

Joe just stroked BB's head and said, "Aw... you poor thing."

"Hi kids," Dad called as he came into the house. Where had he been? "Hi Joe, what are you doing here so early? And BB, how are you doing, cutie?"

Dad's behavior towards BB had changed a lot since she became pregnant. First of all, he always had this grin on his face. Like no matter what went wrong he couldn't be happier. And he treated BB like a fragile piece of glass that could break any minute.

"I had an early day at work," Joe explained. Dad placed a large brown paper bag on the counter.

"Oh, that's nice. BB, I bought you some *borekas* at the *shuk*. I made sure to get the freshest ones there were."

"Thank you, Dad!" BB said, hugging him. "That's just what I feel like eating now!"

That's my BB. Just ten minutes after lunch!

Dad looked happy. "So how you feeling, sweetie? You okay? Can I get you anything?"

"No, I'm fine, Dad. The borekas are great!" BB bit into a particularly crispy cheese boreka. Joe grabbed for one too. Hadn't he just eaten?

"How about a glass of orange juice?" Dad asked. "Or some hot tea? How are your ankles feeling?"

"Oh," BB reached for another boreka. So did Joe. "My ankles are okay. It's actually my neck that hurts me now."

Pinch! My neck suddenly hurt.

"Aw, you poor thing...." Joe said, as he and BB wolfed down yet a third Boreka.

I felt the muscles in my body tense up and pull at me as though I had just fallen from a ten-story building. I tried rubbing my neck, but then my arms hurt, and when I massaged my arms, my ankles hurt.

"Oh honey, here, sit down, relax," Dad ran to get BB a chair.

"That's a good idea. My back is starting to ache."

I keeled over with a sudden sharp back pain.

That was it!

"No! She shouldn't sit!" I jumped off the counter and grabbed the chair just as BB was going to sit on it. "You two should both go home and get some rest!" I said, rushing them out of the kitchen, trying not to concentrate on all the aches and pains I felt. "Yes, definitely go home, put your feet up or something, just get some rest!" Ow! My back hurt so much!

"But we – " Joe began.

But I had already grabbed the bag of borekas and pushed BB and Joe towards the front door. "Yes, you look tired," I said as I opened the door. "And hungry!" I threw Joe the bag of borekas and slammed the door shut behind them.

Dad stared at me in dismay. "Leah, what's the matter?" he asked, concerned.

What's the matter? BB is doing some weird trick to my body! I had to get her out of here before I went numb with pain!

"Nothing, Dad," I said, trying to sound convincing. "But they should rest. Don't you think so?"

"Actually," Dad said, "Since Joe is back early, I thought we should go to the mall together to shop for all the things we planned to get. Raychee and Mom won't be home for another two or three hours, so we'll leave then. Is that okay with you?"

I closed my eyes, willing away the throbbing I felt in my arm. "Sure," I sighed. "Where's the aspirin?"

The whole family was at the mall. We had just finished dinner and were checking out the baby stores.

Suddenly, Raychee opened her mouth very wide and shouted, "OOOH! THIS IS SUCH A CUTE CRIB." She looked pretty funny.

"Raychee, why are you talking like that?" Dad asked.

"UH, LIKE WHAT?" Raychee asked, blushing.

"Is something the matter with your mouth? Why are you opening it so wide when you speak?" Mom asked.

"Yeah," Nathan added. "You look like you're trying to swallow a ping-pong ball while you talk."

"Well," Raychee began, lowering her voice and talking normally again. "Our music teacher at school told us the correct way to speak is to open your mouth wide when you pronounce the vowels. LIKE THIS!"

"Not speak, dummy," I corrected. "That's the way to sing!"

BB was rubbing her neck in obvious discomfort. Oh no, my neck was feeling sore, too.

"Bayla? Honey? How about this one?" Joe asked hesitantly, pointing to a beautiful carriage.

That's another thing. Joe has become more and more nervous around BB since she became pregnant. Always rushed.

"No, Joe. Look at those colors, it will make me look fat," BB declared.

Joe nodded and gave BB a nervous smile.

"But it's not for you," Raychee started, and then as if remembering, she opened her mouth loudly. "IT'S FOR THE BABY!"

"I know," BB scowled at her. "But *I* will have to wheel it and I am fat enough as it is!"

"You think you're fat?" Nathan laughed. "I'm the fat one. I am really, really fat."

Dad always jokes that Nathan is the only boy in the world who watches his weight. Nathan is thinner than any of us!

"No you're not, Nathan," BB complained. "I'm fat. No one likes to look at me. No one even likes being near me anymore."

"We do," my mother soothed, hugging BB.

"That's so sweet." BB leaned her head on Mom. "You guys are always so nice to me. Even though I'm so fat! I love you guys so much." BB stopped sobbing long enough to point to Nathan. "But I am still so much fatter than Nathan."

"But that's only because you're pregnant," Nathan insisted. "I'm this fat without a baby!"

They could do this for hours, and I'm sure they would have if BB didn't have to go to the bathroom.

"Hey, can any of you guys do this?" I asked, twisting my lips to form the letter 'S'.

"No, we can't," Nathan grunted. "Haven't we

been through this already?"

I don't know why, but every now and then I just have to test the limit of my capabilities and find out who else can perform the tricks I do.

"Well how about this?" I raised one eyebrow. "Or this?" I pulled my thumb back all the way to my wrist.

"No, we can't do that, we aren't all circus freaks," Raychee teased.

"That's not freaky, that's talented," I explained.

BB came back with a pizza pie tucked under her arm. "Hey guys, who's hungry?"

We had finished dinner twenty minutes ago.

"This is a nice carriage," Dad pointed out. Dad was the only one of us who could coordinate colors. The rest of us walked around all day looking like we were dressed up for a Purim party.

"It is," BB agreed, "But the baby book says that...."

She never stopped talking about that baby book! Out of the corner of my eye, I saw Joe reach for a slice of pizza.

"Mom, can you do this?" I flared my nostrils.

"What?" Mom seemed confused. "No, honey, I – "

"Mom," Raychee interrupted, "did you know that there is an author called Rudyard? That's what my friend Shahar told me. And I was thinking, why

would someone – ”

“How about this, Mom? Can you do this?” I twisted my tongue.

“Hey, I was in the middle of talking to Mom!” Raychee shouted.

But I had already caught Mom’s attention.

“Leah, that’s very good, you are very flexible,” Mom complemented.

“No one ever pays any attention to me!” Raychee pouted. “I can never get anyone to listen to me!”

Suddenly my father whirled around. “You know what, dear?” He turned to my mother, “I *do* think our children aren’t getting enough attention.”

BB had finished six slices of pizza on her own. And Joe was in the middle of his second slice. BB was rubbing her stomach and groaning as she complained, “I’m full...I can’t move...I’m such a cow.”

She had enjoyed the pizza so much, it almost made me want to eat a slice.

“Why do you think the kids don’t get enough attention, dear?” Mom asked, somewhat insulted.

But Dad was smiling. “Just look. We have one daughter who opens her mouth to the size of an orange when she speaks; one boy who is obsessed with his weight; and another daughter who can *pretzelize* her body!” Dad reasoned.

BB had started crying again. I don’t even know why, and Joe was making a meek attempt to comfort

her. Finally, he bought a pack of potato chips and they ate it together.

"Exactly!" Raychee cried out. "I need more attention. More Attention. MORE ATTENTION!" She pulled on Mom's arms.

"Have we all agreed on this carriage?" BB stopped crying and pointed to a red and blue striped carriage. "Because I really have to go again. And my ankles are becoming too swollen to stand."

Ow. Mine too.

We nodded in agreement to the carriage.

"DAD, I BARELY ATE A THING AT DINNER. CAN I BUY A FALAFEL?" Raychee asked, opening her mouth again.

"What am I? A walking ATM machine?" Dad grunted.

"PLEASE DAD, I'M HUNGRY!" Raychee pleaded, mouth ajar.

"Okay. But only if you stop talking like that. And ask BB if she wants one." Dad handed her some money.

"But she just ate! She can hardly walk, she's so full," Raychee protested.

"I know, but do me a favor and ask her any-way."

"BB?" Raychee called. "DO YOU WANT A FALAFEL?"

"I told you to stop that," Dad ordered.

"Sorry," Raychee apologized. "BB? How about it? Falafel?"

All eyes turned to BB. She started crying again. "That's so sweet of you to offer!"

She was rubbing her left arm. I found that I was doing the same thing to mine.

"Well, do you?" Raychee asked impatiently. I could tell Raychee was *really* hungry.

BB rolled her eyes in exhaustion, patted her belly, and sighed. "Okay."

MONTH SEVEN – Nesting

As the days got colder, my wardrobe got smaller. Raychee was slowly emptying my closet of my favorite sweaters, with the worn excuse of, "Oops, I didn't realize it was yours."

BB still came over a lot, but she was constantly cleaning. And she had always been known for her messiness. While BB and I were talking in my room, I finally exploded.

"Sorry, BB! I draw the line here," I said. "You can clean your house, you can clean our kitchen, you can even clean the bathroom if you feel that you absolutely have to. But it stops here. You CANNOT clean my room!"

"I'm sorry," BB smiled. I saw some tears roll down her cheek as she put my papers back on the floor where they belonged.

"Oh no, BB, don't cry!" I begged.

"It's just...," BB sobbed. "The book says this is called 'nesting.' That a lot of pregnant ladies go through it."

"So, you see? You are normal. Stop crying. Why are you crying?"

"Because I'm so... I'm so...," she stopped crying long enough to think, "I guess it's 'cause I'm so hungry!"

I smiled. What a relief. That made sense. She hadn't eaten in over an hour. I think her hands were beginning to shake with hunger. I hoped mine wouldn't start doing the same.

I had hoped the sympathy pains I must be feeling would pass, but they only felt worse as BB felt worse.

"Let's go over to your house, the kugel we made should be about ready now," I suggested.

I got the chills walking into her house. Everything was so clean, so shiny. It felt so wrong!

I cut us some kugel while BB turned on the air conditioner.

"BB! It's been raining all day! Aren't you cold?" I asked, amazed.

"Are you kidding?" BB started eating. "I'm boiling. But I'll shut it off for you if you want me too."

Pregnancy is such a strange thing.

"No," I sighed. "I'll just wear your coat."

"So, are you excited?" BB asked, taking another

bite. "You're going to be an aunt in a few months!"

"An aunt?" I zipped up the coat and resumed sitting near my sister. "I never thought of it *that* way."

I had only thought of a new baby arriving and ruining the special relationship BB and I used to have.

"*What* way?" Raychee burst into the apartment, followed by Bellvis. She hugged herself. "It's freezing in here! Haven't you guys ever heard of heating? And what's up with the cleanliness?"

"Apparently it's part of being pregnant, BB put the air conditioner on," I explained. "She's hot."

Raychee just shook her head in amazement and sat down with us. "Mom said you guys made a kugel. I want some."

"Sure," BB cut her a piece. "What is that dog doing in my house?" BB did not look very happy.

"I don't know, he followed me here." Raychee shrugged, biting into the kugel.

Bellvis lay down in front of us, waiting to catch any scraps that might fall onto the floor.

"So what were you guys talking about?" Raychee asked again.

"I was just asking Leah if she's excited about becoming an aunt," BB said, not taking her eyes off the dog.

"Oh," Raychee exclaimed, not seeming the least bit surprised at the concept. "I was thinking about that. I've decided I would like to be called Aunt Molly."

"What? You can't change your name!" I laughed.

"Sure I can. I like that better," Raychee said. "You know, it would be much easier if you told us whether the baby is a boy or a girl."

"No." BB shook her head and started cleaning crumbs off the counter. "It's a secret. If I told you, then – "

"Hey," I interjected, "How *were* you able to keep the baby's gender a secret for so long? That's not like you."

BB blushed. "Well, actually..." she lowered her voice to a whisper, even though no one else was in the apartment. "Only Joe knows what the baby is. We decided it would be better if he didn't tell me so it would remain a secret."

"Smart move." I poured us all a drink of juice. BB took the opportunity to wash Raychee's plate.

"Hey, I'm not done with that!" Raychee said.

"Oops, sorry." BB handed the clean plate to Raychee. "Boy, my back is hurting me again," she complained. Uh-oh. I wish she wouldn't say these things aloud. I felt an uncomfortable tingle rise up my spine.

"And I'm sooooo hot!"

Raychee and I exchanged knowing glances.

"Well, I'm already turning blue from *cold*!" Raychee said, showing us her fingernails.

"Raychee, you're wearing blue nail polish!" I exclaimed.

"Well, they're about one step away from becoming *real* blue! And my teeth are chattering, cause it is SO cold in here!" She banged her teeth down against each other, to prove her point.

"Sorry," BB apologized, shutting off the cold air. "Do you know that the book says that newborns like the colors black and white?"

"Like our dog!" Raychee said.

"No," I corrected. "Our dog sees shades of green and red. And by the way, that's my sweater!"

"Oops," Raychee smiled.

We sat and talked for a long time. It was nice. It was sisterly. I wondered again how it would be when BB had the baby. Would we just be able to sit and talk like sisters? I mean, the baby wasn't even born yet, and already it was the center of our conversations.

But I never seemed to get the perfect chance to tell all this to BB.

I thought about how much pregnancy had changed my sister. Suddenly she was always talking, and it was *always* about the baby!

"Oh, it's getting so late," BB said, fanning her face with her hands. She took another piece of kugel but was careful to catch any crumb that fell. "Joe should be home any minute now. Hey! The baby kicked!"

The baby started kicking a while ago, but it was

always exciting to us.

"Wow! This baby is really moving around in here. You want to feel?"
BB asked gently.

She took Raychee's hands and mine
and we felt the head move along her stomach.

How strange.

There is a baby in there.

I am going to be an aunt.

And BB is going to be a mother.

If the pregnancy is so difficult with the baby *in*
there, what will that baby be like when he or she was
out here with us?

"Ooh, that kick hurt!" BB called down to the
baby. I felt my stomach churn.

"I'm hoooome!" Joe called, walking through
the front door and dropping his briefcase on the floor.
BB jumped up to hug Joe.

"Joe, I missed you! Can you massage my fin-
gertips for me? They're killing me!" BB whined, eating yet another piece of kugel.

Hmmm… I wondered if I could get Raychee
to do the same for me.

"Sure," Joe smiled, reaching for some kugel.
"But why is it sub-zero temperature in here?"

"Really?" BB asked, seeming genuinely surprised. "I'm boiling."

BB ran to put Joe's briefcase away and started

rearranging some books on the shelf.

"Man," Joe shook his head, "she won't stop cleaning for a minute."

"You think she's bad here?" I asked. "She tried cleaning my room today!"

Joe laughed. "Well, last night I got up to go to the bathroom and when I came back the bed was made!" he said. "I can't wait 'till this phase passes."

"Don't be so sure, Joe," I said. "You never know what the next phase is."

MONTH EIGHT – Hot Flashes

BB wanted to go to a "Expecting Mothers" convention in Tel Aviv. Joe wanted someone to go with her, because he was so nervous about her.

I volunteered.

Even though my sister was becoming more and more unpredictable, I knew I should cherish the private time I still had to spend with her. The baby would be here before long.

So we had a fun day. BB did most of the talking on the ride there, and I was a little nervous watching her drive. It seemed unnatural to see a pregnant woman behind the wheel. When she turned it felt like the car was tilting towards her. But as worried as I was (and I had to tolerate this for an hour and a half!) I didn't have a heart attack, and we arrived in Tel Aviv safely, although we both had leg cramps when we got out of the car.

I thought the convention was pretty boring, but BB managed to buy four more books and became a member of one of the new mother clubs.

We had dinner and headed back to Jerusalem.

It was quite a cold night, but BB didn't seem to notice. On the way home she put the air conditioner on in the car!

"Wow, I didn't think there would be traffic to Jerusalem this late at night," BB confessed.

"Yeah," I replied.

"Hey, it's pretty cold, isn't it?" BB asked.

Thank God she noticed! "I feel the same way. I was afraid you would still be hot."

"No. I'm cold." I watched her change the air conditioner to the highest level of heat. As she did, her eyes left the road for a brief second, and the car swerved a little.

The car behind us honked a warning.

"That stupid car!" BB shouted. "I wonder who taught *him* how to drive!"

I was afraid to say anything. The mood swings had started kicking in full-time. One second happy, one second angry! I felt bad for the other cars on the road.

Then again, I'm the one *in* the car with her.

I tried to calm her down. "Hey, when's your due date again?"

215

"Leah!" BB scolded. "This is not a good time to ask!"

She was attempting to pass a car. Only she wasn't going fast enough.

"BB... There's a truck coming, you're going to have to speed up if you're going to pass this car!" I screamed, clutching the sides of my seat.

"I know how to drive, Leah!"

HONK! HONK! The truck was getting closer and its headlights were blinding me. Just when I started picturing the light at the end of the tunnel, BB pressed her foot to the gas and swerved past the car.

I gasped. Was I alive? Yes, although I think my heart moved into my ears. We made it! Oh my God! I looked at BB who didn't seem the least bit worried, as though she didn't know we just had a close call.

"Sorry, Leah," she apologized, her voice softer than before. "I didn't mean to yell at you. I just got caught up in the driving."

What is she talking about? Who cares about her yelling? We almost got killed!

"The due date is six weeks from tomorrow," BB said, continuing our earlier conversation.

"Wow," I said, relieved to see that BB had indeed calmed down.

"Yeah. It's pretty soon. It got so hot in here! Didn't it?"

BB didn't wait for my answer.

Most people would turn the heat down a little bit, but not BB. She turned it to the coldest temperature.

It started raining outside. I was thankful that we reached the highway and there were very few cars on the road.

"I bought all these cassettes of cute baby songs the other day," BB told me. "Hey, you want to listen to them?"

"Uh, no. Not particularly," I replied honestly, "I think I'm past that stage."

I didn't have the strength to hear, "There's a hole in my bucket, Dear Liza," while I went into hypothermic shock.

BB started laughing hysterically, and switched the dial back to the hottest temperature.

"You are so funny sometimes!" BB couldn't stop laughing.

I was worried she wasn't concentrating on the road. She was laughing so hard tears were coming down her eyes, and I didn't even say anything all *that* funny!

"You are so great," BB said, finally catching her breath. "I am so lucky to have a sister like you... so... lucky...." BB started crying as she switched the dial back to coldest temperature.

She had to be kidding. This was the ride from hell! My sister couldn't stay in a mood long enough

to see the road, and the temperature in the car was changing so drastically; my body didn't know whether to freeze or defrost! This definitely wasn't the time to bring up the subject of our relationship.

"BB. Don't cry. Please." I tried to pat her shoulder, but she shook my hand off.

"I'm sick of everyone telling me not to cry! I have a right to cry!" She fumed and turned the dial back to the hottest setting.

"I'm sorry. I don't know what's happened to me," BB pleaded. She left her hand on the dial, ready to change it whenever the need arose. "I'm always crying. Either because I'm angry, or happy, or sad!"

And just to prove the point, she started crying again.

This time I decided not to say anything.

BB changed the temperature to the coldest setting again.

I was starting to sneeze. The drastic change in temperature was making me sick.

"And you know," – back to the hottest – "sometimes, I don't even know WHY I'm crying!"

Back to the coldest.

I sneezed again.

"And my head is hurting...," she sobbed.

We should be home, hopefully in an hour, I thought, trying to comfort myself. That is, if we survive this car ride!

I sighed and held my throbbing head. Only six

weeks left to go!

MONTH NINE – Thar' She Blows

The last month was probably the worst. BB couldn't be left alone for a second, and it's as though all the other symptoms got 100 times worse in the ninth month.

Plus, she started walking funny. She wobbled around like a penguin.

Her legs and stomach ached so badly, we had to do almost everything for her. And since she was in pain, naturally I was in pain. I couldn't concentrate on anything but how BB was feeling.

"Here BB dear, I fixed you some lunch," Mom announced cheerily one afternoon.

"Thank you so much Mom!" BB said, happily cuddled into the sofa.

"It's tuna. You like that, don't you?"

"Tuna? No…. All those poor fish…. Dying in order for me to have lunch. How can I eat tuna? I feel terrible! And it will just make me nauseous…."

"Don't worry," Mom comforted, "I'll get you a peanut butter sandwich instead, and how about some nice hot tea?"

"Peanut butter? No…. Can I have a pastrami sandwich? Thanks. And I'm too hot for tea…," BB whined. Mom nodded and headed back to the kitchen.

"Uh-oh!" BB suddenly yelled, clasping her

stomach. "I think I'm going into labor."

Raychee peeked her head in through the kitchen.

"Where are you going?" she asked.

"Labor!" I yelled nervously. "That means she's going to have the baby!"

"Oh, oh, oh!" Dad zoomed into the room, almost pulling his hair out. "Raychee, quick, get Joe on the phone...."

"Ow...," BB groaned. Mom ran to her aid.

"And... Uh.... Leah, you go get the suitcase, I'll help Mom carry BB into the car. Coming, sweetie!" Dad ran to BB.

I ran and got the suitcase from BB's apartment, but no one was waiting for me at the car. Finally I went back to the house.

"Guys, what's taking you?" I asked anxiously.

Surprisingly enough, Dad and Mom were breathing very funny and BB was trying to imitate them. But they were all sitting on the couch and Raychee was looking very annoyed.

"Yoo-hoo, I don't think we want BB to have the baby on our couch," I called to my parents, who completely ignored me.

"Mom said she's not going into Lowboard, or whatever you called it – "

"Labor," I corrected.

"Yeah, whatever. She's got the Bernstein Hex," Raychee explained.

"What's that?" I asked, seeing BB turn red in the face. My parents looked pretty funny breathing like that.

"I guess it's some sort of curse," Raychee said.

"It's – *hee-hee, hoo-hoo* – It's called the Braxton Hicks – *hee-hee, hoo-hoo*," Mom panted between breaths. She sounded like a hooting choo-choo train.

BB raised her hand. "It passed," she said simply, and everyone breathed a sigh of relief.

Mom turned to us. "Braxton Hicks – fake labor. All pregnant women get it in the late months. It's stomach cramps, and you're sure you're going to have the baby, but you aren't really going to have it."

"Oh," Raychee and I said in unison.

"Why were you breathing like that?" I asked.

"Lemaze, that's a special way to breathe when you get contractions," Mom explained, and then looking at Raychee, she added, "Contractions are the stomach pains that push the baby out."

"Well, we're lucky it was only fake labor," Raychee said. "This gives us time to form a new plan. I don't think Mom and Dad will be able to *carry* BB to the car."

What was she talking about? Oh, I got it. "Raychee. Dad didn't mean he would literally carry BB to the car. He meant he'll *help* her walk there."

Raychee seemed more relieved knowing this.

Finally everyone calmed down. Mom nodded at us.

"Okay, sweetie. A pastrami sandwich and a cool glass of orange juice, right?" Mom rushed to the kitchen while screaming: "Leah, go get your sister a pillow, and Raychee, why don't you rub her feet."

"Me!" Raychee shrieked. "I ALWAYS rub her feet! My fingerprints are starting to disappear!"

"Raychee!" Dad called to her, "Quickly rub BB's feet before they start hurting her."

My feet started hurting *me*.

Poor Joe. No one told him it was a false alarm. He waltzed through the front door.

"Oh! What is everyone doing here? I went to the hospital and they told me BB hadn't checked in, so I came to find out what was going on," Joe called out as he came into the house and slammed the door behind him.

BB explained the confusion to him and Joe decided he would take the rest of the day off and hang around with BB, just in case.

"So, watcha' got there, BB?" he asked as Mom brought in BB's lunch.

"A pastrami sandwich," she said in between bites.

Joe walked to the refrigerator and started fishing around for some food. Meanwhile BB had Mom give her a new glass of orange juice without pulp, and Dad circled me nervously telling me the pillow

wasn't *plush* enough and maybe I should get her a blanket as well.

"Raychee, come help me make some eggs for your sister," Dad said, looking for more ways to keep BB comfortable.

Raychee folded her arms across her chest and pulled her shoulders to her ears, clearly stating her objection.

"Come on Raychee, I'll take you shopping later," Mom promised.

She was up on her feet immediately.

A few minutes later, Dad was handing BB a huge plate of scrambled eggs, which Joe helped her eat – although, not before BB asked Mom to season and set it on the plate in a perfect angle to the cucumbers Dad had carefully sliced.

Don't ask me how Mom had the patience for these things. Mom said that's how it is when you're expecting. The one thing I do know is that as far as the family felt, the baby couldn't come soon enough. We were sick of being pregnant! But I was still a little nervous. I never did find the right moment to talk to BB, and I was dreading the day I might end up losing her for good.

We had about two false alarms every day. And we fell for it every time, dashing for the car. Once we even went to the hospital, but they laughed and sent us home. Joe was becoming a nervous wreck and BB was more and more tired.

Then the big day arrived, and wouldn't you know, it was a Sunday.

Mom woke us up late, and told us BB was in the hospital. She would be giving birth within the next 24 hours.

"But she isn't due for another week!" I reminded Mom.

"Well, someone should tell that to the baby," Mom said excitedly. "Because he or she is on its way! Joe and BB have been in the hospital since 4:00 A.M.!"

Dad called Nathan and told him to come to the house to wait with Raychee and me.

"Mom, we don't need a baby-sitter! You didn't have to tell Nathan to come over," Raychee protested.

"I know that. He's not coming to baby-sit," Mom explained. "He's coming because when the baby is born, you should all know at the same time."

"But Mom," I whined. "How come I can't come? Why are you and Dad going and I can't?"

"Sorry, honey," Mom said giving me a good-bye kiss, "But BB doesn't want you to see her like this."

"See her like what?" I exclaimed. "I think I've seen her at her worst in the last nine months! She thinks she can surprise me?"

"Bye, dear," Mom waved, and then she and Dad were out the door.

Nathan came by and we all sat down near Bellvis.

224

"You know," Nathan began. "They say dogs can sense these things."

"Sense what things?" I asked, still feeling a little insulted that BB didn't want me there.

"That a baby is going to be born," Nathan explained. "They can feel it in their bones."

I looked at the dog. He was very happy, lying there with drool coming out the sides of his mouth while we petted him.

"Belle? He can't sense anything," Raychee chimed in. "The only thing he senses is hunger."

Just the word 'hunger' reminded me of BB, and I suddenly missed her very much. I wanted to be with her. All the aches and pains I had been feeling suddenly hurt more than ever. Or maybe it was just that my *heart* suddenly hurt. This was it. BB would have the baby and we would have nothing to talk about anymore. No more *Sunday-Bonday*, no more anything.

The phone rang.

We all jumped up to get it.

I picked up the receiver. "Hello?"

"Leah, sweetie!" The voice on the other end said. "It's Uncle Aryeh! We heard the good news. Mazal Tov!"

"Uncle Aryeh?" I asked, puzzled.

"Yes," Uncle Aryeh said. "You're an aunt! Mazal Tov!"

"No I'm not," I corrected. "BB just went to the hospital. She hasn't had the baby yet."

"Oh," Uncle Aryeh sounded surprised. "Well, your aunt Dorothy just called me. She said she spoke with your uncle Shalom, who spoke with your mother, who said BB had a girl."

How could they know before us? That didn't seem fair! They were all the way in America!

"Well, I don't know what's going on," I said, trying to contain my anger. "But I have to leave the line open in case Mom calls."

"Okay, just tell everyone congratulations from me."

"Will do, Uncle Aryeh. 'Bye!" And I hung up.

"What did he say?" Raychee asked, seeing my disturbed expression.

"He said BB had the baby already."

Just then the phone rang again.

I picked it up.

"Hi, it's Mom," Mom said.

"Mom!" I forgot my anger for a moment. "Did she have the baby yet?"

"Yes. You're an aunt!"

So they did know before us? Oh, who cares! I'm an aunt!

"We're aunts!" I jumped up and down. "We're aunts! This is so exciting! We're all aunts! We're all aunts! Oh, except you, Nathan, you're an uncle! But we're aunts! We're...."

"Yes, it's a healthy baby – " Mom tried to continue.

"Wow! It's a healthy baby!" I screamed at the top of my lungs. "It's a healthy baby! It's a baby! It's a baby!" I stopped.

"Wait Mom, what kind of baby is it?"

"A boy," Mom said, sounding very proud.

A boy! So the relatives got their information wrong. Uncle Shalom must have spoken to Mom when BB was in the hospital. Mom probably told Uncle Aryeh that she *thought* it was a girl.

I was still one of the first to know.

I was so busy thinking, I almost forgot Mom was on the phone.

"Why don't you all come down to the hospital," Mom suggested.

We rushed out of the house, stopping to get some balloons on the way.

BB looked terrible. She was all swollen and tired. Joe wouldn't leave her side. He got very nervous when they brought the baby in for us to see.

"You can hold him," BB offered the baby to Nathan.

"But he's so small. Are we allowed to yet?" Nathan asked, hesitantly.

"Sure, just don't tell the nurses," BB smiled.

"Just be careful...," Joe said nervously.

That's when I realized we weren't the only ones

in the room. Joe's parents were there too. And his sister.

Mom and Joe's mother were hugging each other and crying.

"I want to hold him! I want to hold him!" Raychee reached for the baby.

Joe looked like he was having a heart attack.

"Gently," Dad warned, as Nathan handed the baby to Raychee.

I looked at the baby.

So he was what the fuss was about. The party's over. My sister's a mother. I'm an aunt.

My mouth suddenly felt very dry. I moved closer to BB.

"Congratulations!" I gave her a kiss. "These are for you," I said and handed her the balloons.

"Thanks, Leah," she smiled. "I'm so glad you're here."

I felt like crying. *This baby was going to ruin everything, wasn't he?*

"Go ahead and hold your nephew," BB finally said gently.

I was shaking all over.

"I don't want to drop him."

"Well, you're absolutely right. We don't want you doing that. Maybe we should put him back?" Joe looked at BB, pleadingly.

"You won't drop him," BB assured me.

Raychee glumly handed the baby to me while

announcing, "He is my favorite nephew."

"He's your only nephew!" Dad
corrected.

I looked at the baby. Wow. He was
pretty cute. Didn't look a bit like our side of
the family, but he was still cute.

"Hey, Baby!" Raychee said. "I'm your aunt
Raychee. But you can just call me Auntie Molly."

"Or Auntie Nutso!" I said. I looked at the baby
and smiled. "Hey kid, I'm your other aunt," and
whispered, "The normal one."

I looked around the room. For the first time in
nine months, Raychee seemed excited; Nathan was
actually spending time with us; Mom was looking very
proud; Dad had grown some extra white hairs; Joe
had gained about 45 pounds; and my back and ankle
were killing me.

Nine months, and this was what was left of us.
Was it worth it for the little pip-squeak I was holding?

"So how you feeling, BB?" I asked her quietly.

"I'm a little achy," she began, and I could already feel the pain flow through my body – "But
happy," she continued.

"Yeah, you glad to finally have the baby?" I
asked sheepishly.

"Yes. Very." She leaned close to me. "But I'm
really glad to have *you* by my side."

I was surprised by that remark. It felt like she

had forgotten anyone existed except the baby. "You mean the family?"

"Yes. But you especially, Leah. I couldn't have made it without you," BB explained. "Maybe I was too grumpy most of the time to tell you, but without your help, I don't know if I would've wanted to."

Wow! All that yelling, crying, the extra work, the different phase every day, all the talks of nothing but babies and here she was telling me how special *I* was.

"I can't wait until I'm up for our Sunday-Bondays," BB said.

"You mean we're going to continue them?" I asked, astonished. I figured if we stopped during the pregnancy, it was obvious we couldn't continue once the baby was born.

"Of course. Now that I've had the baby, I don't want to give up my one day a week with *you!*" BB said, as though the thought had never crossed her mind.

I looked at the baby. All in all, he was harmless. He was my nephew. And he was cute. "Maybe we could bring the baby," I suggested, surprising myself even as I spoke the words.

"That's a thought," BB smiled. She looked so happy.

Was it all worth it?

Looking at the family, and then at my sister, and at my newborn nephew, I felt the pain ooze away

from my body. I felt good.

Yes, it was definitely worth it.

Mom was right.

At that moment, there was no way I could have felt closer to BB.